I0670919

J. D. Clockman

RETURN TO ODIUM

London
Jetstone
2018

A *Jetstone* paperback original.

ISBN 978-1-910858-09-7

Cover design by The Ever-Shifting Subject.

This is a fiction. The events it depicts are
entirely imaginary. Only two of its
characters have any real-world
equivalents, but the events
pertaining to them
are also
made
up.

Chapter One

When the moment came, it sounded more like the crack of a rifle shot than an explosion.

On the high crest of the hill that was Red Road, far from the milling crowd of hundreds strung out across the waste ground, down on the flatland on the other side of the high rises, Robert McNamara had been standing alone for fifteen minutes, in a silence he had never known here, which only the detonation finally broke. The roads all around had been closed to traffic on account of the planned demolition and he had had to make his way here on foot. He followed the countdown from a position on the pavement opposite the little store he had never gone into as a child because it was the shop next to the Protestant primary school on Red Road whose name he could not now remember. There was always a news-agent's near a Glasgow school, placed to tempt sweet-toothed kids each morning as they clutched their yellow threepenny bit or silver sixpence, not knowing until the last few moments, when inside the very emporium itself, if the large glass jar they would point to would contain pear drops or kop kops or liquorice string or, on cold days like this, dummy cigarettes which one could actually seem to be smoking. Most of his early walks to school, he recalled, were prefaced by this eager anticipation of confections, which were poured and weighed and folded in a little white bag which was then stuffed into pocket or satchel, provisions against the trial-by-boredom of the coming day, not to be savoured until morning playtime, a long fifteen minutes of sugar-fuelled relief and delight.

There had been a similar shop near St Martha's, his own Catholic primary school, which he could see now if he turned all the way around and looked north, its squat brown bulk extending across the ridge of a hill yet higher than Red Road, about half a mile distant as the crow flies. What was the name of that sweetshop? Gaffney's? Mc-Gaffney's?

He had never known the name of the store he now waited near. Catholic kids and Protestant kids did not mix in the days of his childhood. There was usually disorder if they did. The school on Red Road was eventually closed and became a community centre just after he had left Glasgow aged twenty-one, and the remaining McNamaras had been decanted from the high-rises to a house on the edge of the city after an asbestos scare and a fire which had killed a boy in the tower across from their own. They had transformed the block Mc-Namara had lived in, first into a YMCA, then into accommodation for nurses at Stobhill Hospital, and then – irony of unbelievable ironies – into a hall of residence for students at Strathclyde University. The store had successively reinvented itself in parallel. On brief trips back home, McNamara had witnessed it as an Indian takeaway, then as a hairdresser's, and the last time he remembered it as an off-licence. Now it was a pizza shack.

He reflected that there must be others in the vast throng in the offing down below who had also once lived

6

here and who had, like him, come to see the architectural execution. Did they think of themselves as victims of the condemned, or were they grieving family? He had no real wish to find out. The idea of intermingling with them, of trading brief details or anecdotes of a time past, in fragmentary exchanges which would have resurrected in him that also long gone, more vulgar version of the Glasgow voice he still possessed, had never seriously arisen in his mind. He had no wish to pretend to share with people whom he knew were essentially strangers. They had no doubt mainly chosen their spot because it offered the best view of the occurrence as a spectacle. From where they stood, they could see the entire row of four nearly one-hundred-metre-high columns that would fall simultaneously that afternoon, and it would be thrilling, sensational, the nearest thing to the Blitz that any of them, most likely, would ever experience outside a movie.

These buildings had, for a while, been legendary, the highest residential blocks in the whole of Europe at the time of their construction. McNamara, however, was watching just one tower, and he had to be on this side of it, because it was on this north-facing façade, nearly two hundred feet in the air, that he had lived all those years. Imagining as all educated people do that he was somehow singular, thinking that for him the buildings' end would have a meaning whereas for the others it would be merely a happening, he felt he had come to confront the moment rather than consume it, in a kind of reckoning. He had even overstayed nearly a whole week since his father's cremation in order to do so.

He had suffered one shock already. When they had moved into the apartment almost exactly half a century before, in 1967, in the January, after his early years in a

Springburn tenement with an outside toilet and a single metal bath which passed daily among six tenancies, he had been just tall enough, when he ventured onto the verandah, to look through the gap between the balcony's protective panel barrier and the metal banister which topped it. The view thrilled him. Any view would have thrilled him, because their previous abode had had no view at all, never mind any spot inside from which fresh air could be breathed or laundry windily dried. The verandah looked east along a straight treeless avenue. At hundred-yard intervals, on the right of this unadorned grey ribbon, stood the other three behemoths of Petershill Drive, and he took some pride in the fact that they were not quite as tall as his. Nonetheless, everything was still massive, gigantic, thrusting skyward greyly in defiance of all nature, and he loved it.

It was a view but no vista, however. At the end of the avenue, where it rose in a slight incline, extended a truly monstrous slab of three similar tower blocks facing him directly, all combined in one structure, like colossal dominoes glued together on their longer sides. It had the effect of a huge horizontal door, permanently closed and barring all sight of everything beyond it. It was so enormous and forbidding that it occluded the sun that rose behind it until well into every morning.

His grandparents, his father's mother and father, had lived in the centre section of this slab. Once McNamara had asked his father – a betting man, horses, who watched weekend racing on TV – what a furlong was. His father had taken him out onto the verandah, upended a plastic basin and perched him on it so that he was a few inches taller and could see further down. He gestured along the line of tarmac avenue by wiggling a finger to and fro. "That's a furlong," he had said. "From here tae granny and grandad's is a furlong." And then his father had said something else of the kind he often said in these brief moments together, smiling as he did. "They lived here before us, but no' *furlong*."

There was no furlong now. The momentous slab was already gone. Six months before, in phase one of the planned destruction of the entire housing complex, the planners had brought it and an identical structure not far from it crashing down into two small continents of rubble which spilled at ground level across the grassy areas and playgrounds and the furlong McNamara had frequented as a boy. He had watched the razing of his grandparents' erstwhile home from every angle YouTube had to offer, with a detached curiosity which had not prepared him for the actuality of standing on the spot and coming to terms with its real absence. A week earlier, on the morning of his father's funeral, he had found himself staring east, from a distance at the end of Avenspark Street, along the line of what had once been the furlong, and seeing nothing. It was like looking at an old friend whose head had suddenly been cut off. The February sun was weak, but it was the first time he had seen that sun in this place at that hour of day in his entire life, and it was blinding.

The countdown ticked away. McNamara took out his phone and held it away from his body, his own old tower block captured in its vertical video frame. He would watch the decisive moment on screen, and felt oddly protected from the likely impact by the veil the phone seemed to provide. He counted up again from the bottom storey of the block, from one to seventeen, and kept his eyes grimly fixed on the four windows on the left of the seventeenth floor.

The detonation was precisely on time and, at this distance, he saw its effects a second before he heard its report. It took place in all four towers simultaneously. On the screen he saw sharp, violent horizontal exhalations of dust and smoke spume out at various levels on the lower half of the building before the short clap of the explosion reached him, and to the left of the phone he could see the other three blocks move and shift in a blur and begin to dislodge from their moorings. He could not but be distracted by them for a second, looking to the left of the phone to see them totter and begin to assume strange angles. He snapped his eyes back to the device, making an effort to hold his arm and hand still, and saw that his own block had started to move too, so that he could no longer locate floor seventeen. He watched the great skyscraper destabilise and begin to sag. It seemed to wilt and give up the ghost and now there was a slow upswirl of dust and debris climbing the screen, accompanied by an onrush of sound reaching his ears, like a slowly gathering wave before it crashes, and suddenly there was a patch of over-exposed light from the sky at the top of the screen as the roof of the building started to lower with its fall. He was aware, to the left of the phone, of the emergence of great patches of light as the other three pillars dropped cleanly away, like men before a firing squad, except for the noise they all made, which grew from a sibilant sigh to a voluminous rumble which extended and extended much longer in time than he had imagined it would, as if it were all happening in slow motion, or as if it were taking place on a planet where the hold of gravity was weaker, eventually becoming a deafening roar for a few seconds before the beginning of a truly terrifying cacophony of dissolution and collapse. But his ears told him one thing while his eyes, fixed to the screen, told him another. The building on the phone screen was still falling and crumpling, but it had not gone completely like the others, it seemed to be offering some stubborn resistance, like a living thing, like Orwell's elephant, crying out in pain, down on one knee, but refusing to die with just one shot. Then it disappeared from view on the screen as brown and grey dust billowed skyward from all directions, engulfing everything that could still be seen of it.

McNamara lowered the phone and stood silent and rigid. The surge of noise withdrew as quickly as it had come and he thought he heard cheers and whistles and claps reach him from the now hidden crowd below. But he could not be sure because his ears were ringing. The dust cloud rampaged up the hill towards him, fast and menacing, so that he feared it might swallow him up, and he even held his breath in anticipation. But it lost all its thrusting energy thirty feet inside the safety barriers and slowly, slowly, over many minutes, it gradually thinned out and receded.

As it cleared, a still vast shadow became discernible behind it, tilted at a weird, calamitous angle, about half its original size, seeming almost to be swaying slightly in the still, cold afternoon. His own tower block had not completely gone. For the first time in decades he felt again a tingling sense of pride in its superiority to the others. As the smoke thinned and dispersed and his thoughts cleared a little with it, he whimsically felt that his scenario was a little like Charlton Heston's at the end of *Planet of the Apes*, but instead of raging despair he felt a quiet triumph that not quite everything had yet gone down into oblivion and disintegration.

At last he could see the entire remains. His building seemed to teeter on some brink, daredevil, defiant, angled grotesquely leftwards, at maybe a twenty-degree tilt. He started to count the storeys, this time perforce starting from the top. On the right side of the building he counted sixteen surviving levels. On the left he counted thirteen – and a half.

He did not know how long he stayed rooted there. After a while he set off in something like a fugue state. Four streets intersected at the top of Red Road. The way downhill was obstructed by security barriers, but he tried the other three like a lost dog at any crossroads, making his way along them spontaneously, then stopping and retracing his steps and ending back where he started, staring hypnotically for moments on end at the teetering tower block. At last, as if inspired, he simply decided that he had nowhere specific to go and opted to wander.

There was a large recreational area to the north behind fences and chained gates. It had once been a vast expanse of three or four asphalt football pitches – they had called it simply "the red ash" – but many years ago it had been locked off with bright eye-catching notices on display speaking of danger and land subsidence. These were now grimy and faded. Apparently there was an old forgotten mine underneath the entire surface that young boys had happily played football on for years. But McNamara remembered from his youth that fences around here were simply barriers through which one sought entry via a hole, and it did not take long for him to find one. As the wintry day began to darken, a half moon already low in the clear cold sky, he found himself strolling aimlessly across the terrain of his childhood sporting adventures for the first time in fifty years. He had forgotten all about this place.

Eventually he arrived at what he remembered was a disused railway cutting. The line had been axed by Dr Beeching around the time McNamara had been born. It had been used in the First World War to bring wounded servicemen to Stobhill Hospital, but he remembered it as a curious untended scar on the landscape, with two foul-smelling and rubbish-strewn tunnels at either end. He went right and headed for the smaller tunnel, and would have gone through it had he not been distracted by the lights of All Saints Church, off to the left, which he had attended as an adolescent. He climbed the incline towards it and heard from afar the sounds of an organ and singing. It was a Sunday and this must be the beginning of five o'clock mass. The hymn sounded puny and ridiculous from a distance, so he skirted the church grounds and found himself on Broomfield Road and, giving in to an absurd whim, a few hundred yards later, he turned into the Broomfield Tavern, a grim council-estate pub which had been his father's local, but into which he had never ventured.

He emerged after two hours of silent drinking and observing younger men playing pool and watching football on the largest television he had ever seen and speaking to one another in coarse loud voices that sounded always just below the level of shouting. He carried in a bag by his side a half bottle of blended whisky, the best the place had had to offer by way of a carry-out. Though the worse for wear, he knew where he was going, and plodded off up the gentle slope of Rye Road, then right into Scotsburn Road with its refurbished but still mean tenements, then left into the gentle downward decline of Ryehill Road. This route took him past All Saints School, a secondary establishment for the baby-boomer generation that had succeeded his in the early sixties, and which he had therefore never attended, but which he had watched being built, brick-by-brick, or rather breeze-block-by-breeze-block, on his daily bus journeys to St Roch's in Townhead. All Saints too had vanished, at least in the incarnation in which he had known it, its population having shrunk from the seventeen hundred it housed in the mid-1970s to a mere six hundred today, the imposing main building that had once been there having disappeared and been substituted by a titchy little thing which sat meekly in the still expansive original grounds.

On he went, feeling like Gulliver in Lilliput. The two-room library at Rockfield Road, the terminus for the number 55 bus, simply wasn't there at all anymore, and nothing else was in its place. There were just green tufts and brown scrub. Right at the dual carriageway of Wallacewell Road, left at the similarly wide and steep Northgate Road, past the small Church of Scotland and jerry-built Sunday school at the bottom of his father's garden, and then huffingly, puffingly, left into Northgate Quadrant and, after a drunken fumbling for keys, he entered the house where his father had literally seen out his life. McNamara strode with urgency to the toilet to placate his disorderly prostate, and finally slumped into the bolstered armchair in which dad had had his only and final heart attack, not being found until four days later, the neighbours alerted by the smell, the TV still on, with many flies on his body already (as the woman from upstairs had felt the need to report).

McNamara sat in the darkness and drank the whisky dry, straight from the bottle. At nine o'clock he suddenly realised that he was too drunk to drive and that his intention to leave in the early evening had been overtaken by bibulous events. He stumbled into the nearest bedroom, his father's, crashed and seemed to wake one moment later, though it was now two in the morning and he had a headache. The bedroom still reeked of his father's cigarettes, but this was preferable to the still ineradicable stench of rotting flesh to be encountered in the living room. He went into the small bathroom, took one look at the still unwashed bath and decided, no, maybe not, in fact, definitely not. He turned off the electricity and gas at the mains, checked all the taps, was thankful that he had already packed and put his suitcase in the car, left the house, locked the door, stepped into his Ford Mondeo and turned the key in the ignition.

He was not yet fully sober and so, ten minutes later, it did not feel all that unusual to be standing in his old bedroom, panning the flashlight of his phone around the remaining three outlandishly-angled walls, with hundreds of thousands of tons of concrete tottering directly above him, and the dark shard of an immense steel girder protruding through the roof above where his bed used to be. There were indeed always gaps in security fences around here, and he had readily found one close to the block. He gave little thought to night watchmen. If there even were any, he doubted that they would come within three hundred yards of the now-leaning tower of Petershill, and what would they do if they encountered him anyway? Prosecute for trespass? A fine? At his age, what did he care? He wouldn't even bother to talk his way out of it or feign the mad Professor. But, sure enough, there were no watchmen. There was nothing to protect anymore.

He was surprised he could get right into the skeleton of the base of the building. He had come only for a closer look, imagining that there would be a miniature Munro of wreckage barring any possible entry. But in fact the colossus had come apart in the huge iron-rod-reinforced segments of which it had been pieced together, like a scaled-up fallen Jenga puzzle or a disarranged Stonehenge. Some of these hunks had split into smaller pieces, but these were still so enormous that, now at rest against one another, they formed a crazy maze of awnings and jagged arches and lurching tunnels that even a fat man like McNamara could wend a way through by stooping and bending and being careful of foot.

The kitchen at the end was entirely gone. His parents' bedroom, to the right of it, was ground down almost entirely to the roof. Only a small angle of what had been his sister's bedroom remained, and when he shone the light inside all he saw was grey-white blank and broken stones. But about three quarters of his own bedroom, towards the building's central staircase, remained. He had had to stoop sharply to gain entry, but once inside he saw that the walls and roof sloped upward and away, and he was even able to stand upright in part of what remained.

The actual spot, he reflected, meant nothing, was all wrong. He had not lived at ground level. Now nearly forty years since he had left it, he could expect nothing here that spoke to him or of him. There was no floor at all, never mind a carpet. He assumed that the boulder-like forms which crowded the space were what remained of it. At the far end from where he had gained entry he saw a mangled white door that he knew instantly was not the same one he had handled all through his second decade of life. That left the walls and the roof. These were damaged and holed, but not so much that he could not imagine The Incredible Hulk pushing the building upright for a few moments, righting the angles, so that he could re-envision the room where he had grown as a youth in a succession of oft-repeated acts. Here he had done his homework, discovered masturbation, drawn a moustache on his upper lip with a black felt-tip pen and stood with a tennis racquet in front of a mirror while the radio played, read books, fumbled with the bra-hooks of two or three girls he sneaked home while everyone was out, often sat with one or two schoolmates playing records, put up posters, smoked secret cigarettes and even more secret dope, gazed out at the distant Campsie hills beyond the city. Here had been the bed, there the small desk and lamp, over there the paraffin heater that reeked, and later the Calor gas heater that caused so much condensation, the chipboard wardrobe, the chest of drawers with his Sanyo cassette player on top. Here he had repeatedly listened through the wall while his sister, aged fifteen, was willingly fucked senseless by her older boyfriend. Here, latterly, he had insisted on his privacy and imperiously excluded all three other members of the family. Here one morning he had opened the university letter, his back to the closed door and his heart pounding, which had proved to be his exit visa from this room, and eventually Glasgow, and Scotland altogether.

He sat on a piece of smashed concrete and bowed his head, his fingers to his temples, his back to the room. Great drunken tears welled up and splashed on his shoes. His mother, ten years dead. His father, ten days dead. His sister, who despised him and he her, not met with this century, except at two funerals. His ex-wife, on husband number three. His two sons, grown up, flown the nest. Rachel, abandoned by him just weeks before. And now, this ruined fortress from which, when he raised his tired eyes, there was no longer that distant, hopeful view, but merely a mound of lop-sided, broken stones, crowding together in the half moonlight, like relics in a vandalised cemetery.

*

He drove. West along Petershill Road, left onto the long drag of Springburn Road, where the National Carriers main depot had been, where his mother had worked as a secretary, now a Tesco. On down to Townhead, St Roch's miraculously still there at the end of Royston Road, and not far past it the Royal Infirmary, where both his mother and his grandfather had died, where he had last seen both of them alive. He was aiming for the M8 east but instead he chose to take it westbound to Charing Cross, where he came off and drove down past the Hilton Hotel, built on the very spot where his father had been born, then back and left along Woodlands Road, slowly up and over and down the hill of University Avenue, the reading room on the right where he'd spent so many hours, the mock-gothic spires on the left where he'd taken so many classes, the entire place spookily empty under moonlight, right at Byres Road, past Hillhead Library, where he'd worked one summer, delightedly finding himself the only lad alongside nineteen slightly older girls, up Queen Margaret Drive, into Ruchill, where his father had lived as a boy, now Bilsland Drive, what had his father's street been called? He struggled for the name but without it he would not find it on the GPS. He kept going on what proved to be a circular detour, left into Hawthorn Street, past the Cowlairs depot where his father had been a British Rail wages clerk, right again onto Springburn Road, down once more into Townhead, St Roch's, the Royal, crassly hiding the cathedral as always, the M8 east, signs for The South.

Motherwell flashed up, and he suddenly remembered Bruno. Bruno. Another Catholic, they'd been indivisible friends at Glasgow University for three years, Bruno studied languages, his father was also Irish, but Bruno had been born in England, Warrington, wasn't it? His family moved to Wishaw when Bruno was in his teens. Damn it, he even remembered Bruno's school, Our Lady's High, Motherwell, and yet he couldn't remember his own father's Ruchill street name. Bruno was the last person in life that McNamara had truly looked up to, a walking multilingual thesaurus even at twenty, a face like a movie star, everyone thought he was Hispanic. Unlike him, Bruno had not meekly assumed a Scottish accent as a way of fitting in but maintained his suave, defiant Englishness, though he had a way with all kinds of voices and mimicry and could do all shades of Scottish and English and Irish and Welsh, leaving everyone around him with their sides splitting. They'd lost touch in McNamara's last year, when Bruno went off to Paris on his year abroad, because when he came back McNamara was gone, off to Oxford to do his D.Phil., and the next thing McNamara knew, it was ten years later, and Bruno was on TV and radio all the time, with a changed name, a bloody comedian, not a stand-up, an impersonator, doing The Establishment in different voices, satirising Neil Kinnock and Michael Heseltine and David Coleman and Paul McCartney and everyone else you could think of who was famous and male, and not just British but foreign too, given his languages, part of a popular sketch show, then he got a show of his own, and he was even more hilarious, gut-wrenchingly, lung-challengingly mirthful and politically biting all through the Thatcher decade. McNamara used to watch his Saturday night show with his young sons and they'd go into school and tell their friends their dad knew Bruno, though that wasn't his name anymore. Then, yet another decade on, no, no, more than that, fifteen years maybe, McNamara was coming off the set of *Channel 4 News*, he'd been doing a live interview about some political event, something they thought a Politics Professor was right for, when the studio manager thrust a mobile phone into his hand, said there was a call for him, and it was Bruno. Bruno had been watching and he knew the studio manager personally and he called her right there and then and asked her to catch McNamara as he came off set and McNamara was overwhelmed and they spoke briefly and Bruno wanted to meet again but he was leaving the country next day to do something in America, though he'd be back in a month or two, and three days later McNamara opened *The Guardian* and found out Bruno was dead in a Las Vegas hotel room with too much crack cocaine in his veins. He wasn't even brought back home. They scattered his ashes somewhere in Nevada.

Lesmahagow, Hangingshaw. Lockerbie, where the remnants of the Pan-Am plane came down. England now beckoning, silhouettes of hilltops becoming lower in the moonlight. Ecclefechan, birthplace of Carlyle, the sign said, but which McNamara remembered as the spot where he'd once passed a car ablaze, and a woman screaming by the side of it, bawling someone's name into the roaring white and yellow flames, and he'd stopped, and got out, and made to go back to the scene, but just then a fire engine and an ambulance screeched up, hoses were turned on, he saw that he was not needed, and he turned around, and drove off again, never knowing quite what had happened here.

He stopped at Gretna Green. There was a twenty-four-hour truck stop and he thought to venture in for some coffee, but he closed his eyes for a few moments and, an hour later, woke gasping and spluttering from a dream of his father burning in a Ford Mustang in the Nevada desert, Bruno standing beside the car, doing an impersonation of Ronald Reagan, with an atomic bomb going off in the distance behind him, and the ludicrous steeples and minarets of Las Vegas falling like ninepins through the heat haze. It took him some moments to realise where he was, so contrasting was it. It was freezing cold. It was dark. He was still just in Scotland. His head ached dully, but it was not so bad as before. He found himself suddenly sobbing and beating both his fists on the steering wheel of the Mondeo. He took out his phone and looked at the time. He lurched out of the car, pulling his overweight body with difficulty, unzipped his trousers, pissed in a ditch, and got back in.

He drove into England. Carlisle, Penrith. The M6 would be quicker, but that way Warrington lay. Bruno's family, McNamara realised, must just have got out of Warrington, turned left, driven straight up the M6 and A74, and turned right into Wishaw after two hundred miles, simple as that. But it did not seem a night for direct routes, whatever the time. He took the A66 east and kept his foot down, careless of speed cameras or ice. What did it matter? What did anything matter now?

Brough, Bowes, Scotch Corner, the A1 south. Racing towns that reminded him of his father: Catterick, Wetherby. Why did everything mean something, why did every place name bear associations now? McNamara had once hired a Toyota Hilux in Bangkok and driven for hours and hours with his elder son, north, through places no tourist went, tiny little towns and villages that looked not much different from what they probably looked like a century ago, the signs all in Thai, hard to tell a hotel from a big house, no English spoken anywhere, no pictures on wayside food menus, everyone they met staring at them with incomprehension, and he knew if he had been alone it would have been alienating, but with his son with him it felt like a hilarious adventure to both of them, all the way up to the Burmese border, and then along it, down the border with Laos, a crazy three-week road trip, a different, stranger place every night, the stranger the better. Yet now, when he was on his own, nothing was strange, everywhere was impregnated with significance or remembrance or familiarity of one kind or another, and he wished it would stop, he wished he knew little and had experienced less. It was as if he had exhausted the world and it had nothing left to give except repetition and dread recycled in bad and worsening dreams.

Pontefract, Wentbridge, Doncaster.

The moon was no longer visible.

Tickhill, Blyth, Ranby.

Tuxford, Newark, Claypole.

The sun was up when he reached the Bruntham turn-off, and saw the first sign for Odium.

Chapter Two

Two and a half hours later, James Redman found himself
in a slightly awkward colloquy with Vice Chancellor
Archibald Spooner. Redman had been in the comm-
odious office of Odium's Vice Chancellor on the ground
floor of the Trump Building only twice before, but the
difference in the appearance of the room now could not
be ignored. Gone was the sleek modern business-
signifying furniture in black and grey that had marked the
style of the late Sir Evan Covet. In its place were heavy
burgundy drapes with rich golden tie-backs, baroque red
leather chesterfield sofas and a rich, deep-pile scarlet
carpet. Red seemed to alternate with green, despite the
old maxim forbidding their admixture. There were
numerous lime-shaded Emeralite desk lamps, and taller
standard lamps with shades with the marbled hue of
watermelon skins and further gilted hanging cords, all
very rococo. Two Italianate statues of nude males, slightly
smaller than life-size, stood on plinths in bright window
recesses, their likewise slightly smaller-than-life-size
penises facing all visitors over each shoulder of the Vice
Chancellor, whose desk was so positioned that he always
had his back to them.

The current incumbent of the office presented himself in similarly flamboyant and slightly antiquated style. He appeared to be in florid health and was not overweight. He wore a paisley cravat and an open-necked shirt, over it a navy blazer with bright gold buttons from whose breast pocket peaked a deep red handkerchief, sporting grey slacks pressed to a fine crease, with white socks and shiny black tassled loafers below. On his head was a resplendent mane of smooth hair, browny-blond, luxuriant for a man in his sixties, long but expensively cut, touching the right shoulder of his jacket, towards which it was swept over, so that his left ear was always visible. He was marked with a tan deeper than any which could reasonably have been sustained by the British climate. Below his mouth of full pinkish lips was a dark brown mole, on the right of his close-shaven chin, although the rest of the face was smooth, almost glistening, a little soft. He wore a bracelet on his left wrist and on both hands several rings, but none of them indicating marriage. His fingernails were roundedly manicured and very clean. As a polished assemblage he too was difficult to overlook.

They had proceeded past introductory small talk. The third person expected in their meeting was a few minutes late and, apparently to do no more than pass the time, Spooner had begun, in an affable drawl, to seem to try to tease out from Redman some details of the scandal surrounding his own predecessor's demise.

"But you were in the thick of it, no?" he nudged gently, in a deeper voice than his soft features suggested was likely. "You were one of the people whose offices the Union claimed he bugged."

"I was," Redman replied laconically. "But no bugs were ever found."

"You think Dr Poon made it all up? Surely not? She said Professor McNamara came into her office and found the very bug that had been planted there, and showed her the two others. She took a photograph of all three, she claimed."

"I wasn't there," said Redman, shifting a little in his seat. "Is this what you want to talk to both of us about?"

"Oh no, we have much bigger fish to fry!" Spooner reassured him enthusiastically. Then, more pointedly and worldly-wise, tapping his nose, he added, "I got the strong message that there are stones it is better to leave unturned, don't you agree? Nonetheless, this was a lot of rum stuff to take place in a British university, no? Sort of things, if they happened in a novel, you'd shake your head at in incredulity."

Redman smiled gently at what seemed a subtle reference to his own credentials as a Lecturer in English Literature. "Last term required a lot of suspension of disbelief, it's true."

Spooner sat back, beamed, and looked about to continue when, without a knock, the heavy door was opened and McNamara stood in the entrance, a slightly flustered young secretary a step behind him. Spooner at once arose and beckoned McNamara towards him while simultaneously waving the secretary away. "It's alright, Eloise, no need for formalities, we've been expecting Professor McNamara."

Spooner glided across the carpet and extended his hand as the door closed softly. McNamara took it briefly and said, "Excuse my slight lateness. I was travelling through the night."

"Not at all," said Spooner. "I'm glad you could make it."

Redman looked at McNamara with a silent internal

shock. The older man seemed the opposite of the colourful surroundings. His thinning hair was greyer, except on his face, from which all traces of his beard and moustache had been removed. His face looked curiously younger, but also gaunter and weaker. Without its previously permanent hirsute surround his mouth appeared smaller, the lips thinner. He was dressed completely in black – suit, tie, belt, shoes, socks – except for a plain white shirt which stuck out at the belly. His eyes were tired and rheumy. He was a little stooped and his shoulders sagged. His movements towards the proffered chair were slow and deliberate. He seemed to take no interest in the novelties of the redecorated room.

Re-assuming his seat, which seemed more like a throne manqué, with a hint of Charles Rennie Mackintosh in its high back, Spooner said breezily, "Robert McNamara, a name to conjure with, eh?"

McNamara looked back through heavy eyelids. "I was born before the Kennedy administration. A mere coincidence."

"But I wasn't aware that you were Scottish, like me!"

McNamara again made a lugubrious reply. "It would appear that you have to be Scottish to be the Vice Chancellor of Odium, yes, but in fact that rules me out, as I am actually Irish. I grew up in Scotland, however, hence the accent."

Spooner smiled smoothly and said, "Glasgow?"

McNamara nodded slowly.

"Which part?" asked Spooner. "I'm from Giffnock myself."

There was a pause in which McNamara seemed to study the new Vice Chancellor for the first time. At last he said, "Balornock."

Spooner looked puzzled. "Balornock? I'm not sure I

know –"

"If you grew up in Giffnock," McNamara interjected bluntly, "you wouldn't."

After the briefest of pauses, with the air of a man who knows how to restitch an unexpected hole in any conversation adroitly, Spooner said, "We must look at a map and you must show me sometime."

McNamara nodded expressionlessly again, his eyes closing and opening as his head was lowered and raised.

"Now," began Spooner, and then was distracted by a notification sounding from the smartphone on his desk. He looked at it briefly. "Excuse me, gentlemen, I can't really ever turn this thing off in case something urgent arises, and so it may beep and blip occasionally while we are talking, but the good news is that all the sounds are customised for certain types of message, and so I will only need to react to it if what we hear is a train whistle or, in the worst possible scenario, a foghorn. The twenty-first century, eh? Remember when things were simpler?" He nonetheless flipped open the cover of the phone so that he could see its screen.

"Okay," he resumed. "We have about twenty minutes for me to try to explain some new and exciting directions we are taking here at Odium and how I hope you two gentlemen may be able to play a significant part in them. Will you bear with me while I expatiate a little, leaving some time for your questions after I sketch out a few ideas?"

Redman looked uneasily sideways at McNamara, whose demeanour gave no cause for reassurance, as he simply continued to stare straight ahead at Spooner.

"Sure," Redman said. "Feel free."

Spooner smiled graciously, clasped his beringed fingers together in front of his face, tilted his head to one side so that it was no longer hidden behind his praying hands, and began.

"I am an historian by training, as you may know," he started. "But I do not intend to dig too deeply into the, er, *history* of what took place here last term, of which you know much more than me. I am assured, however, that you both played a major part in saving this institution from outright disaster, a disaster that would, had the present government gotten its way, have affected the whole HE sector very badly. Of that Dr Asterisk has convinced me in the most fulsome terms. In fact, he paints you both as the heroes of the piece.

"Now, I have been made aware also of your, er, *history* in the University, the trades union activities, your joint disaffection from all that, and for good reason, but also the unique knowledge you have of how a twenty-first century university like this one works, and not least your familiarity with the particular people here, by which I mean not just the academic staff but also the senior management team, as well as the administrative organisation, and so on. Not to put too fine a point on it, you know the ins-and-outs of things I have only begun to grasp in the mere month or so I have been here. But please note that I see myself as coming from the same neck of the woods as you. By that, I mean, my entire professional life in academia has been in the Arts, Humanities and Social Sciences, like you. Not only that but, politically, I see myself as a liberal. I am not sure if you would describe yourselves using that word, but I am certainly no right-wing conservative of the Sir Evan Covet kind.

"Now, we sit in an institution that is eighty-one per cent science if we go by research funding income, a little less than that if we go by student numbers. It has, in the past, under Covet, pretty much followed the money, in my view to the detriment of disciplines like ours, which have been relegated in the last twenty-five years to having little more than the status of icing on the cake, and a very thin icing at that, icing which has been forced even to pay for itself, against all enlightened common sense. We all know that Theology and Philosophy and the Classics cannot reasonably be expected to operate at break-even, never mind a profit. Indeed, from what I have gathered, many of the people down the hill in the sciences would gladly get rid of the icing altogether, were it not for the fact that they receive constant reminders, or maybe kicks under the table, to the effect that a cake is not really perceivable as a cake if it does not have icing to decorate it. These are the people who have largely been allowed to run this institution heretofore.

"But they shall be allowed to run it no longer. They all scrambled like cowards – the senior managers among their number, I mean – to escape the blast zone of the Evan Covet blow-up. Needless to say, since his suicide, though I shall name no names, many of them have crept back inside the circle, seeking reinstatement. But I have ignored all of them. They showed no loyalty to him or, worse, to the institution. They proved that, when the breach was agape, they were not prepared to leap into it. Whoever was going to close up the wall, it was not going to be them. They were fairweather friends to the University of Odium. Their loyalty was proven to be merely to themselves and nothing larger. Yet even your enemies do not say that of you. Even Dr Asterisk, who left me in no doubt at all how much you opposed Covet, made it clear to me that, when the chips were down and the government was making its opportunistic move to compromise the entire sector, you acted to save the day when you could easily have let the havoc be wreaked."

Spooner was interrupted by two short pips from his smartphone. Seeming slightly annoyed, he glanced at it, then pushed it slightly further away from him.

McNamara asked, "How much did he tell you?"

Spooner shook his head and gestured dismissively with his hand. "We agreed to keep it vague. It seemed best."

Redman said, "But none of this is about the future. You are talking about the past."

"Yes," said Spooner, "thank you for reminding me. It was intended as context merely. I will come to the main point. I intend to put an entirely new managerial team in place. I intend, over the next three years, to create a virtuous economy in the Arts, Humanities and Social Sciences which will raise the proportion of their activities in the University to forty per cent of the total instead of their current twenty per cent. And I would like your help."

"A virtuous economy?" said Redman sceptically. "That sounds like a euphemism."

"From twenty to forty per cent in three years?" whistled McNamara. "The only way you could possibly do that is to downsize the sciences. But you cannot divert science funding to other purposes. No one is going to support that, not even us."

"Oh no, please, gentlemen, let me be clear. I am not playing with statistics. There will be no diminution in the sciences. It is simply that I intend to focus on a programme that concentrates all new effort on doubling the activity – in student numbers, research grant income, staffing levels, and investment in other resources – outside the sciences, at least on this campus. I cannot promise it for the campuses in China or India."

Redman sighed. "A new focus, a new emphasis, new

efforts? Well, of course, they would all be welcome. But doubling the activity is pie-in-the sky without a major, and I mean major, cash injection."

Spooner looked across the desk and let a broad smile cross his face. "Yes," he said.

McNamara looked for the first time at Redman. Redman eyed him back. They returned their gazes to Spooner.

McNamara said patiently, "When James uses the word *major*, Professor Spooner, he doesn't mean modest local pump-priming of the kind the University might be able to re-allocate from its own discretionary funds."

Spooner was still smiling beatifically. "I know," he said. "He means systemic, across-the-board investment of an absolute kind. He means totally new money. And lots of it."

His phone chirruped and he glanced at it, picked it up for a few seconds, read something on the screen, then put it down again. His eyes alighted once more on the other two men.

"How," he said, "does eighty million pounds over three years sound, forty in the first year, twenty in each of the two years to follow?"

Redman blinked several times.

McNamara frowned and raised his hand to his head. "But that's, that's..." He was doing some rapid calculations. "That's a hundred and fifty per cent of my own faculty budget in the same three-year period, and Social Sciences is the largest of the three non-science faculties. Across the three faculties that would be something like a sixty per cent increase in expenditure."

"If you include the administrators," Spooner rejoined. "Actually, if we can find a way to streamline the administration, to centralise it into one body to serve all three faculties, instead of each of them having an independent administration of its own, allowing that new administrative structure to grow in staffing modestly but not unduly, the estimates I have commissioned reckon on it as something more like a seventy-five percent increase. Most of the money could be spent on new academic staff, new programmes, two or three new buildings, and scholarships."

There was a pause, while Spooner looked slowly from one to the other, seeming to savour the moment, though not too vaingloriously.

McNamara scratched his head.

Redman sighed again, but his sigh was a little different from the one before. It had something more positive sounding in it. "Well, I have a couple of questions," he said.

"You bet," said McNamara. "Like what's it got to do with us?"

"And where's the money coming from?" added Redman.

Spooner nodded. "Okay. As I shall explain, the answers to both questions are linked. First of all, what has it to do with you? Well, I need people I can trust. I need people who might engage wholeheartedly with the opportunity to make this place a properly balanced university again, rather than the technocratic market-chasing machine it has become, the business-in-all-but-name that it's been reduced to, about which you have complained and protested for many years to no avail. You are not the only people who fit into this category of trustworthy individuals, but you seem to me among the few. For example, Professor McNamara, have you ever thought of being a Pro-Vice Chancellor?"

McNamara coughed a dry laugh. "There are some

desks I won't cross to the other side of."

Spooner pursed his lips in seeming slight dismay, then relented and brightened a little. "Okay, I understand that. Then how about Dean of your own faculty?"

McNamara frowned. "My faculty already has a Dean."

"Yes," said Spooner, "but her term as Dean finishes at the end of this budgetary year. The new dispensation would not begin until the new budgetary year on August first. You could replace her then. And, Dr Redman, though you are not a Professor and I could not offer you such a senior managerial position, I could make you Vice Dean in the Faculty of Arts, and give you a leading role on the committee that would plan for the new growth and implement it. Moreover, I could relieve you both of teaching for the next three years in order that you may concentrate on this vital work."

He let these proposals hang in the air between them. The silence was broken by repeated *toot-toots* from his phone. Spooner breathed out sharply in exasperation. "Gentlemen, excuse me, it's the train whistle, second in seriousness only to the foghorn. But it happens more than you'd think. My colleagues have a more heightened sense of emergency than I do after the events of last term. I must take this, but I should be only a few seconds. Forgive me."

He got up, but he did not leave the room. Instead he crossed to one of the bay windows, speed-dialled and looked out over the lake, his hand on the head of one of the naked male statues. He held the conversation in discreet tones, but he made no attempt to prevent them from overhearing it. He spoke genially and professionally, as he had done throughout.

"Yes, Nigel. Your text. A situation, you say? Can you give me more detail? Okay. But I am in an important meeting right now. Yes, Professor McNamara and Dr Redman. We should conclude soon but I don't wish to interrupt it for something that will probably turn out to be a false alarm. Please gather as much detail as you can and ask Eloise to call you when we're done. Then you can come and see me directly after. Yes. And thank you, Nigel."

He hung up and returned to his seat behind his desk.

Redman said, "And the money?"

"Ah, yes," said Spooner, and the first hint of awkwardness crept into his expression. "Thereby hangs a tale. But it's a tale I am not responsible for starting. I can only write its conclusion. Its original author died before he could complete it. I mean, of course, Sir Evan Covet."

"Oh," said Redman.

"Oh oh," said McNamara.

Spooner smiled again and raised his hands, his palms facing him, in what at first looked like a gesture of supplication but then, as his arms went higher and his eyes also turned upwards, seemed to be taking in their entire surroundings, asking for them to be considered.

"This building," he said, "in fact, almost every building on campus, used to be called something else. We, or I should say Sir Evan, traded those old names for cold hard cash. He was very good at it. I saw the figures in the minutes of a University Council meeting. In total he raised about eleven million, just from renaming our real estate, virtually magicking money out of nowhere, from nothing, from companies and wealthy individuals who wanted their trade mark or moniker on concrete or, in the case of this one, limestone. Now, what I am about to tell you need not remain confidential, because we are officially going public with it at noon, in about an hour. This building, this was the jewel in the crown obviously, and for this Covet got a cool million from –"

"The Donald," said McNamara, rolling his eyes.

"Well, ahem, yes, but you know, it's hard to knock, I think, really. A million is about ten years of non-clinical professorial salary including superannuation, or fifty non-science scholarships for a year, and for what? For nothing? For simply redesignating a heap of lifeless stones? There's a certain amount of brilliance involved in a deal like that."

"If," replied McNamara, "you are happy to live with the ideological associations, which Covet clearly was. Not to mention remaining silent, and making your own science academics remain silent, when Trump built a golf course on a site of special scientific interest in Scotland."

"I agree," said Spooner, "but these are not problems, I'm afraid, which have died with Covet. You know that it was just a minor tax write-off, the renaming of this particular pile, just a marginal excess from Trump's British resort operations, little more than small change for public relations purposes? When was that, six, seven years ago?"

"Two thousand and nine," Redman said.

"Well, Covet kept on courting him once he'd got a foothold. Remember, Trump has Scottish ancestry. Covet didn't get into golf for nothing, apparently. It was all about Trump. And again, think, this is a man who has given his name to an entire university and not just buildings, even though Trump University is not a real university. And they genuinely got on, he and Covet. Now, this was long before anyone had any idea that Trump would run for President, never mind win. Covet was just hanging on in there for whatever he might get for us, for Odium, but when Trump won the Republican nomination Covet really ramped up his own woo-Trump campaign.

I've seen the file. Covet was down there at Number Ten with David Cameron at least once, asking him to smooth out some of the wrinkles between HMRC and Trump's British companies, pointing out the kind of patronage that might arise for British education, or at least for Odium, from a less ruffled relation between them. Whether or not it worked with Cameron, who knows? It's hardly something that would be in writing. But it wasn't just Cameron. There was a whole host of lesser ministers and under-ministers Covet badgered too. Did you notice, after Cameron resigned, that Theresa May said nothing critical of Trump? Covet was among the people who wrote advising her to stay silent, just in case, *just on the outside chance* that Trump might win. And all through that time, Covet was talking to Trump, writing to him, even apparently meeting him quietly for half an hour when Trump came to Scotland during his election campaign. The burden of it seemed to be that Covet persuaded him, in order to win the votes of all those white supremacists and evangelicals back home in the US, that he would have to say things that would piss off the entire liberal world and damn near every foreign government that mattered, and that what he had to do if he was by chance successful was have a strategy in place to buy back favour with that same disgruntled world afterwards. And it seems to have worked. In fact, Trump liked the idea so much that he moved on it even before he won the presidency. His people talked to HMRC, they negotiated a future three-year deal on the taxes from his British operations, he threw in another few million on top, he already had a connection with Odium, after all. It's all a bit opaque but, I am assured, totally above legal challenge. The irony is that Covet died only a few days before Trump won the election. It was me who got the call, from The Donald personally, ten days after he was sworn in."

McNamara faltered, swallowing hard. "You ... you..." His voice trailed off drily.

"I think what Robert is trying to say," piped up Redman, coming to his rescue, "is that ... you are seriously telling us that Odium is about to receive a donation of eighty million pounds from...", and he could not help but raise his voice somewhat for emphasis, "...the new President of the United States, *Donald fucking Trump*?"

Chapter Three

They left Spooner's inner temple, and walked without speaking along the corridor. Nigel Asterisk appeared on cue from the door of his Registrar's office, almost as if he had planned deliberately to encounter them. As they drew near he nodded in acknowledgment. Redman returned the gesture and slowed, but McNamara kept walking.

"Amazing news, no?" Asterisk said to them both, looking askance as McNamara brushed past.

"Er, yes," said Redman, still moving, but more slowly. Caught between a wish to exchange words with Asterisk and a need to close the widening gap with McNamara, he found himself walking backwards. "Totally a cause for amazement."

Asterisk changed direction and moved towards him, following him with some urgency. "So what do you think? Are you in?"

Redman looked over his shoulder. McNamara was gone, already out in the Trump Building quadrangle. He jerked his head in that direction. "We have to talk."

"Okay," said Asterisk, halting. "Call me."

Redman nodded and turned around, hurrying

through the exit, past the tub of flowers into which, though he did not know it, Cannon Buckrack had thrown his cigarette on the morning of his first meeting with Asterisk the previous September, and out into the middle of the quad, where McNamara stood waiting for him.

It was bright and chilly outside, but the air was still, with no breeze. On such days the sounds in the flagstoned quad were amplified and echoing. The centre of the Trump Building was not busy, though Redman could see a familiar figure striding purposefully through the east arch in their direction. This was Elfyn Dethbridge, the Deputy Registrar, whom McNamara called "Buttons" and told anti-Welsh jokes about. Dethbridge saw Redman from afar, over McNamara's shoulder, and nodded with strained courtesy as he approached.

"Well," Redman said to McNamara, "what did you think of that?"

"Pah," said McNamara without reserve, "he's a *fucking gaylord.*"

At this resoundingly voiced condemnation the balding head of the passing Dethbridge, which had been nid-nodding towards the entrance from which they had just emerged, twisted around on its stalk, scowling. He caught Redman's eye.

"Oh," Redman called to him in attempted apology, "not you, Elfyn. Someone else."

This explanation did not seem to have the desired assuaging effect. It made Dethbridge simply glower more intensely, or as severely as it was possible for him to do. In truth his face mimed the behavioural contortions he thought might indicate reproach, but to the dual sources of his sudden offence these were read as the mere semblance, and no more, of the drooping retreat of a shrinking violet. It appeared that Dethbridge had no time to stop, whereas in fact all his instincts were telling him to move away faster, though he managed to put on a show of exaggerated stiffness caused by enhanced affront.

McNamara had noticed Dethbridge only when Redman hailed him, a few seconds before his stiffened form disappeared into the bowels of the building. "Ah, Buttons. He must be going to see Baron Hardon. You know, Buttons was once stranded on a desert island for three years –"

"You've told me that one, Robert."

"Ah. Pity. Well, it's just gone eleven, maybe it's the time of day for him to take a lovin' spoonful from Spooner."

Redman squinted at the older man in the cold late morning sunshine. "The Buttons routine I get, Robert. But the sudden homophobia? Where's that coming from? About one in twenty of our colleagues seems to be gay and about one in ten of our students. There's a lot of it about, haven't you noticed? You even get your LGB with T and an added letter every week these days. It's become entirely respectable. Isn't one of your own boys gay?"

"Ah, well," said McNamara. "That's different. He's a perfectly decent gaylord, not a *fucking gaylord*. Just as there are some hetero-women who are loveable sexy minxes and there are others who are just filthy poxy sluts. There're many shades of gay."

Redman smiled. "I wasn't asking what you thought of Spooner. I was asking what you thought of what he had to say."

"Ah, fuck him," said McNamara contemptuously. Then he tutted and started on the more rounded response that seemed required. "Tell me if I'm wrong. He wants to co-opt us into some quasi-managerial positions in order to help him make a hard sell. He needs us to endorse the

Trump brand and he's prepared to bribe us each with three teaching-free years as a reward. But what he's really after, though it was all between the lines, is help in dealing with the anticipated Union backlash and maybe a battle from the scientists too. As soon as this becomes public knowledge, in an hour or so, Poon – hah! our other resident gaylady-in-chief – will be building barricades in the air and having visions of herself in the newspapers again, playing Dame Avril Scargill. She'll be calling emergency Union meetings by this afternoon and there'll be an unholy return to another odiousness-of-Odium phase of the kind we just got out of. The scientists will probably join forces with her out of their usual greed and massive sense of entitlement. Why would we want to get mixed up in that kind of thing again?"

"Granted," said Redman. "But he didn't seem so bad. It looks like he's insisted that, though he'll take the money – and how can he *not* take the money, *seriously*? – he won't have it dictated to him how he'll spend it. And he wants to use it to create a massive upswell in the human sciences, not the technocratic ones. Sure, he's caught in an absurd contradiction, given where the money is coming from, as well as what he says about his own moderate politics. But he's prepared to buck the obvious trend. There'd be fat on our slice of the land again. That seems worth compromising on a few principles for, no? There can hardly be another university in the country where they could even dream of such a thing."

"It depends," McNamara replied, "what those principles are. You perhaps forget, James, my near-terminal isolationism. I'm close to out-Crusoe-ing Crusoe. I'm not sure I even need a Man Friday these days. How do you compromise on that? Or, to change the island analogy, while Prospero in there is about to conjure up a storm that will also inspire Sycorax-Poon, I don't fancy being Caliban to either of them. It sounds like you do."

"I'm just saying," Redman soothed, "we should think about it and maybe talk more when the dust of the announcement has settled. He's given us until the end of the week." He looked anew at the man before him, and gestured to his dark attire. "How are you, Robert?"

McNamara heaved a sigh. "I'm tired. I was driving all night. I need to go home and get some sleep."

"How was the funeral?"

"That seems a while ago now. It's already going down into ... I got through it."

"And Rachel?"

There was a pointed pause while McNamara stared straight at him.

"Fuck Rachel," he said.

They parted, and Redman sauntered into the ground floor School of English by the opposite entrance. He strolled down to the middle of the corridor and turned left into the School Adminstrator's office, through an empty assistant's antechamber which buffered it from the traffic of the main thoroughfare. There he found Lorraine Quant, who was on the telephone at her desk by the window, but she extended her free hand, and he took it and squeezed it gently. Then she withdrew it and pointed to a seat. He watched her with her back to him, gazing over at Asterisk's office opposite, as she wound up the call.

"Yes," she was saying. "Again. That's the fourth working day in a row, only two of the absences notified. No call from him this morning. He just didn't show up, *again*. Professor Matthews had his meeting with the

British Academy people at eleven and I had to log on to Yunus's computer to check that he'd organised the coffee at the start and the catering at twelve-thirty. That's where I found it. Right there on the desktop. I opened it and looked at it and it seemed to be what it said it was. Professor Matthews hadn't arrived yet and so I called you. I remembered that training session we did on this kind of thing and I followed the steps. I didn't know where else to go for advice. I hope I did the right thing. You have? And what did the VC say? I see. Elfyn? He's coming over now? Five minutes? Okay, I'll wait for him. Thank you. Bye-bye."

When she hung up and turned to him she appeared troubled, but they both had got used to not prying into each other's professional business. It made for a simpler life.

"We still on for tonight?" he asked.

"Well, yes," she said, distractedly. "But I think it's going to be a rough day. I... I...".

"Trouble?" he prompted.

"It's Yunus."

"Not in again, I see?"

"Well, it's worse than that. Come and look. But we'd better be quick because Dethbridge is coming over soon."

"Yes, I saw him in the quad. He thought Robert had outed him and was a bit cross."

She led him out into the front office and closed the door and turned the lock.

"Robert's back?" she said. "How is he?"

"He seems in bad shape. Dented. Cynical."

She crossed to the computer on the assistant's desk and flicked the mouse to activate the screen. Then she pointed with one elongated finger at a particular icon.

Redman leaned in closer.

43

"Fark," he said, as was his wont with her. "And that is what it is, is it?"

She nodded. "It does appear to be an ISIS training manual, yes. Asterisk said no one else should open it, so don't, but I did when I first saw it. How to make explosive from fertiliser, how to pack it in a suicide jacket, how to choose targets, how to use an AK47, how to conceal knives on your person and the best way to use them to kill, how to conduct yourself under interrogation, and so on. A couple of hundred pages, with diagrams and photos. The kind of thing we are meant to call in immediately, and so that's what I did."

"Fark again," he said. "But it doesn't seem like him at all. We all have him down as a rather gentle soul, a bit of a New Age leftie, in fact, you know, the soft kind. Doesn't he run with a dance troupe or something? Hardly a jihad man. I mean, leotards?"

"Yes," Lorraine said. "You think you know someone, right? But actually that wasn't what shocked me most." She pointed to another icon next to the one for the ISIS training manual. "Open that and you'll see what I mean. I thought it meant 'US' as in 'USA' but I figure it just means 'us'. You'll see why when you look at it. I'll retreat while you do. I don't want to see it again."

She went back into her own office and Redman took the seat before the screen. He clicked on the video file, and recoiled almost instantly at seeing Yunus's close-cropped, well-groomed beard and moustache wrapped around a dark, stiff penis in porno point-of-view perspective, with muffled sounds of excitement off-camera. A male voice was hissing, "Yeah! Thassit! Take big mouthfuls of cock! All the way down yer throat! Be a good little boy and lemme see me dick disappear inter yer face!" It did not take long for Redman to grasp that Yunus

44

appeared to be a consenting, indeed enjoying, participant. A moment later he understood that the movie had been shot by the fellated cameraman, no doubt using his phone, from the very office chair he now occupied.

"Jesus Christ!" he exclaimed, and leapt up. *What the fuck*?"

He turned around. Lorraine was at her desk again, both hands on either side of her head, over her ears, her eyes closed.

"Did you tell Asterisk about that too?" Redman wondered.

"Not yet, but they're going to find it. I can't delete it, can I?"

Redman pondered a moment, regarding her shock. "I suppose it's not that much different from what we –"

"It's altogether different," she snapped. "For one thing, I don't have a cock. For a second, I don't do it while you are sitting in this chair, in my workplace. Nor would I at all if … if you said such filthy things."

Redman grunted. "And, yes, and … he's a practising Muslim, no?"

"You think? I wonder. I'm beginning to see it as just an excuse to bunk off twice during the working day for a bit of extra me-time."

Redman laughed. "Or *he*-time."

"Those so-called prayers had a habit of taking up to an hour, not twenty minutes. It didn't seem to matter how many times I talked to him about it, he just disregarded me. But then I am a woman, aren't I? Oh, he was never unpleasant, quite the opposite. He had a sweet way with him, everyone agrees on that, even me. All this lot down the corridor, all your fellow academics, they all seem to love him, are forever chatting to him while the work waits and waits. Even the Head of School, oh yes, Matthews seems to think he's a little darling. So I hesitated a long time. But to tell you the truth, it had already got to the point when I was about to press the nuclear button on him, especially after his absences this last week. I've had nearly a year of this crap, tolerating him, expecting him to buck up. It got beyond a joke. I've been the one getting all the blame for his complete lack of care in his job. I didn't quite expect it would end this way though. It makes it easier."

Redman dawdled a little, as he often wanted to do in Lorraine's orbit. "Well, at least the man in the hot seat didn't seem to be Dethbridge," he laughed. "That wasn't a Welsh accent."

"Speaking of whom," she gathered herself, "you had better leave."

They kissed briefly.

Redman went out into the empty corridor and closed Lorraine's door, crossing to his own office directly opposite. As he fumbled in his pockets for his keys the double swing doors at the end of the corridor were thrown open and a tall, hatchet-faced man, powerfully built, wearing a long brown overcoat, strode briskly in his direction. Flanked as he was by two equally tall uniformed policemen, he might as well, Redman fancied, have had CID stamped on his forehead. It took a few seconds before Redman noticed Dethbridge scurrying to keep up behind this surging, triple-breasted human wave of law enforcement.

The detective stepped straight up to Redman. "The School Adminstrator's office?" he demanded.

Redman pointed silently across the way. The detective nodded and rapped forcefully on Lorraine's door. As he waited for it to be opened, he indicated wordlessly to both constables that they should assume a position on either side of it. Redman saw Lorraine's face briefly in the gap that opened up, at which point the plain clothes man turned and raised an open palm to halt the pursuant Dethbridge.

"No," he said decisively to the Welshman. "I need to talk to Ms Quant alone. I shall call you in when we have finished."

He disappeared inside, leaving Dethbridge stranded outside Lorraine's closed office, looking from one to the other of the constables.

"Do you know how long he will be?" he said to them.

One of them shook his head silently, with lower lip protruding, then took his eyes off him and stared straight ahead.

Dethbridge turned to see Redman standing in his open doorway. "Er, James, do you mind?"

"Do I mind what?"

Dethbridge raised a hand towards the interior of Redman's office.

"You want to come in?" Redman guessed.

"Yes, thanks," said Dethbridge, moving forward. "And can we leave the door open?"

"My door is always open, Elfyn," Redman grinned. "Would you like coffee? I have an Italian espresso machine. I even have biscuits. We runners need to maintain our calorie intake."

"I don't run," said Dethbridge.

"I can see that," said Redman. "I meant marathon men like me. My 'we' was not meant to include you. It was more royal."

Dethbridge frowned testily. "Since I'm here," he said, taking a seat, "since I'm waiting –"

Redman interrupted. "Why are you here, waiting, Elfyn? What's afoot? You came in on the jet stream of the

Flying Squad and then got blown out of it."

"Oh that," Dethbridge fluttered. "I can't say, it's hopefully nothing. Dr Asterisk sent me over to keep tabs on these officers."

"You don't seem to be doing that. You could have insisted when he waved you away. You surely want to know what he's asking her, whatever the hopefully nothing is about?"

"I, I ... I can't discuss it with you, James. But since I'm here I *would* like to discuss what happened earlier, in the quad. I won't take it, you know. I don't have to stand for it."

Redman finished spooning coffee grounds into the machine. "Stand for what?"

"For that kind of insult."

"What kind of insult?"

"Professor McNamara's. I am just doing my job, James, I should not be subjected to –"

"But I told you then and there," Redman replied, "it wasn't you he was referring to."

"Oh," said Dethbridge, "it just so happens, by sheer coincidence, that as I am passing –"

"But why would you think, automatically, that he must be referring to you?"

Dethbridge halted in his speech, seemingly a little caught out by the question.

"Milk, sugar?" said Redman, deliberately making it sound as if he were using a term of endearment.

"Just a little milk," Dethbridge replied.

"Ginger nuts or jammie dodgers?"

"No, just coffee will be fine."

Redman handed him a small cup and saucer and took a seat on the other side of his desk.

"As I was saying, there are University policies, you

know. And it was in a public place."

Redman grimaced slightly in disagreement. "Well, it was a private conversation going on in a public place which was entirely empty apart from me, him, and latterly you. Robert had his back to you. I can assure you that he did not know you were there. And as I said, he was not talking about you. So there was neither intent to offend you, nor should you be offended, as you were not the object of his comment."

"Well then, who was?"

Redman sighed. "Why don't you ask Robert?"

"If," said Dethbridge, "he was referring to the only other person it is likely he was referring to, then the disrespect is even worse."

"Really?" Redman sat up, a little interested now. "It's more disrespectful if said of one person than if said of another? How's that?"

"On account of his position."

"Whose position?"

"The position of the insulted person."

"But how could he be insulted if he couldn't hear it?"

"That's beside the point. A person of high standing should be able to demand respect."

"I see," said Redman. "So, it was more disrespectful to say it of that other person in his absence than it would have been to say it of you in your presence, because of that other person's, what, his *rank*?"

Dethbridge thought about his own logic for a moment and then, hesitantly, answered, "I think so."

"Well, that's an argument I'll have to consider for a bit, especially as we don't really have *rank*, as such, around here. It's a university, Elfyn, not the military or even your Odium police force out in the corridor there. Relations are meant to be collegiate."

"Collegiate?" Dethbridge snorted. "How collegiate was Professor McNamara's conduct?"

Redman groaned. "His conduct? Since when did two informal words spoken privately in an off-the-cuff exchange amount to something as formal as *conduct*? That's a bit officious, no? And I say again, why don't you take this up with Robert? He's the one who said it, not me."

"Because, because," Dethbridge stammered, "he's impossible to talk to. He has always been impossible to talk to. He is utterly uncompromising, even contemptuous."

"No, that's not true," said Redman. "I'll grant you he often gives the appearance of *impatience*, but not to those who know him. You do realise that he is something rather special in his field, and that with a research assessment coming up he's an asset to the University and his School? Other places have been trying to poach him, but he has stayed. People with his kind of *rank* often appear to be a little Olympian and forbidding."

"That gives him no special licence," Dethbridge insisted. "It gives him no right."

"But didn't you just say that men of higher rank demand, what did you mean exactly, greater regard?"

Dethbridge sat in frustration, as if feeling led into a conversational impasse.

"What you could do, as you seem so over-vexed by the matter," continued Redman, "is you could go and tell the person you think he was referring to what you heard him say, and let that person decide what to do."

"That's preposterous!" exclaimed Dethbridge. "How could I? How could I possibly?"

Redman smiled kindly. "Then maybe let it go," he suggested.

Dethbridge did not seem satisfied. Rather, he made as if to exercise his anguish yet further in speech, but the attention of both men was at that moment distracted by events in the corridor.

A young man, presumably a student, had appeared before the sentinel constables and was engaging them in conversation; or rather, he was interrogating them, and they were refusing to answer.

"What's goin' on 'ere, mate? Wotcha doin', uh? What's happenin'? Standin' there?" He spat questions at the two officers, turning his head from one to the other, so that Redman could see his face in profile. The policemen ignored him resolutely. He was olive-skinned, but his accent was unmistakably east-end Odium, and the voice seemed a little familiar to Redman. "Cat got yer tongue, what? Gonna stop me if I try ter go in?"

This last question seemed so pointlessly rhetorical that the officers' continued refusal to answer was a given. One of them tapped quietly on Lorraine's office door. By this time Dethbridge was on his feet and moving agitatedly towards the corridor, but the young man had now disappeared, moving outside the field of view offered by Redman's framing doorway.

Redman got up and followed Dethbridge, stopping at the threshold and looking curiously along the corridor to the left. The student had not departed, but was loitering ten feet away. He had taken out his phone and was making a call. Dethbridge seemed to be trying to intervene with the constables, but was as neglected by them as the young man had been, because Lorraine's door had opened and the sizeable, grim-expressioned detective had emerged. One of the officers leaned in to him and spoke in his ear, nodding in the young man's direction. The CID man stepped a foot or two into the passageway and regarded the student stonily.

"'Ey, Yunus, 's'Faraj. Yeah, man, you not in? Am at yer office, bro'. Der's cops 'ere, so you stay away, man, they's guardin' yer office, outside it, two of 'em –"

He went on talking with ostentatious loudness, but the detective had obviously decided that he had heard enough. He turned to the uniformed officers and twitched his head in Faraj's direction.

"Take him," he said. "I'll have to call in and have the other one picked up."

The two constables instantly moved in unison like a pair of large guard dogs acting on instilled command. They swept either side of the nonplussed Dethbridge, one of them pushing away the weak barrier of his one outstretched arm so forcefully that Dethbridge was virtually spun round in a pirouette, then stood rooted to the spot as he watched the spectacle which unfolded.

So did Redman.

Within seconds one officer had taken Faraj by an elbow and the other had closed a fist around his phone, plucking it from the young man's hand before seizing his remaining arm.

"Oi, what da fuck?" cried Faraj. Entirely ignored, his voice began to rise to a shout. "*'Ey, ya fuckin' leave me alone, yeah? Who the fuck do ya fink ya is? Gerrof, ya cunt! Ow!*" He was struggling as they pinned his arms behind his back and one of the officers magicked a pair of cuffs from somewhere on his person.

Alerted by the noise, doors began to open along the corridor and some of Redman's fellow academics' familiar heads bobbed out. Students who had been beyond the double doors at the end of the corridor opened them cautiously and gazed wide-eyed at the arrest from afar.

Faraj began appealing to these witnesses. "*Hey, check it out, peepul! Nazi fuckin' state at work! I was doin' nuffin'. So why d'ya fink that is, yeah? An innocent Muslim? Look at these cunts doin' their shit right where ya work! In a fuckin' university!*"

He was writhing in the officers' grip, leaning his body forward and trying to drag them along behind him, but he was held back by their strength, pitched at an angle at which he would otherwise have naturally fallen, like a cartoon character running into the face of a powerful wind.

The two constables seemed practised at what they were doing and were not in the slightest flustered, though they gave the sense that they were becoming a little impatient.

One looked at the other and said, "Down?"

The second took an instant to nod and reply, "Down."

"*Fuck yer mothers! Fuck yer pets and yer daughters!*" Faraj was now upbraiding them in a high-pitched scream. "*Ow, yer breakin' my fuckin' arm, pig! Fuck yer auntie and yer uncle!*"

One of the policemen put a hand on Faraj's back and pushed him forcibly while the other flung an arm under his chest to ensure that his landing was not too heavy. The latter then applied pressure to his head, keeping his cheek against the floor, while the former put a knee in his back and expertly cuffed him. The only part of his body that could now move were his lower legs, his heels flailing helplessly a few inches off the ground.

"*Wotcha doin' now, eh? Ya see this, peepul? Ya see what they did! Do not turn away! Bear witness ter the totalitarian British state in action! Wotcha gonna do, boys? You gonna shove a truncheon up me arse? Is that it? Or ya need some dick down yer throats and this the*"

53

only way ya can get it? Go on then. Turn me over, take down me pants and eat me meat! Swallow that shaft, ya Fascist cocksuckers!"

It was at this obscene explosion of gay-baiting that Redman recognised in what context he had heard the voice so recently before.

Chapter Four

There was no teaching at Odium on Wednesday afternoons, which were designated as a sports period for the students and a meetings period for the staff. Thus, two days later, Redman found himself in the School of English's staff common room, seated in an unobtrusive corner of a large improvised square of desks, regarding most of his colleagues with dispirit and dismay. He had positioned himself, as he always did, across the room from Lorraine, in part to maintain their habitual pretence of distance between them, in part so that they could exchange meaningful looks throughout the usually tiresome and sometimes absurd proceedings. But today Lorraine, her face framed by the neat lines of her short page-boy haircut, sat tensely upright, in a bright white blouse and navy skirt, by far the most pointedly dressed woman in the room, surrounded as she was by those of her kind scattered around in dowdy floral frocks or jeans worn with capacious, bosom-disguising t-shirts.

The six student representatives were shuffling out before the meeting's reserved business began. They had, in the ordinary business session just concluded, raised one or two tentative questions concerning events of the preceding forty-eight hours but, delicate millennials that they were, paragons of obedience to authority that they wished maturely to show that they aspired to be, they did not prickle, they instigated no further friction, when told by the Chair that these matters were still confidential and could for now be discussed only in their absence.

The Chair was Professor Bernard Matthews, the sixty-six-year old Head of School, a D. H. Lawrence specialist who refused to retire and who subscribed to the view that the purpose of Literature was to promote what he was happy to call "roundness of life", a term he glossed, when challenged about it, by saying no more than "it requires explication only to those for whom it is not already an apprehended experience manifested in concrete feeling". Redman eyed him with some foreboding at the manner in which he was likely to handle what was to follow.

Matthews was a small hunched creature, who since middle age had cultivated the weathered appearance of an outdoors man, largely by avoiding sunlight and patiently acquiring anxiety lines on his face, his main access to anxiety being immersion in the works of DHL, which, he earnestly believed, forced greater existential demands on their readers than anything else the world conceivably had to offer. He had published on no other writer in his thirty-five years at Odium, and the endless stream of Lawrenceana which he had steadily released into the gutters of low-status academic journals and paperback introductions and coffee-table biographies had made him a modest name in a contracting field. DHL donated much to his private as well as his professional life. He wrote pseudonymous poems based on Lawrencean tropes and motifs which suffered punishing rejections from small magazines, was passionately absorbed by videos of copulating animals that he found on YouTube, and was a member of a spiritual paganism sect whose headquarters, fittingly enough, was in Taos, New Mexico, and which he visited at least once a year. Despite the self-declared roundness of this life which harnessing himself to DHL had contoured for him, he nonetheless bore certain grudges heavily and sometimes without disguise. He resented his parents for not giving him a name like Rupert or Lilly or Oliver but instead provoking others to think of him, when first introduced, as the diminutive *doppelgänger* of a boorish one-time Norfolk turkey farmer. In order not to repeat this error he had named his one daughter Ursula, only to experience a depression which lasted for years when she unaccountably changed her name, on her eighteenth birthday, to Lucy. He owned one of DHL's jackets, which he had paid a lot for at auction, and draped it over the back of his seat whenever he wrote on Lawrence or, as now, when he chaired meetings. When Lorraine Quant had asked him within a few weeks of her appointment why he carried "that grubby old Oxfam thing" around with him, he had taken an instant and abiding dislike to her. He lived in permanent puzzlement as to why the several offers he had made to other men for a literal *blutsbrüderschaft* had never been taken up. He had, of course, married an older German woman who was twice his size.

With the students safely out of the room, Matthews *ahemmed* and began to intone reedily, peering through his bifocals at a spot on the floor before him and seldom looking up to make eye contact with the assembled staff.

"Well, now," he said, "I am sorry that we have to come to that part of the meeting in which the febrile outer world, the drab domain of politics and the state on this occasion, trespasses upon our scholarly insouciance. As I think you all know, our much-liked School assistant administrator was arrested and incarcerated by the local constabulary on Monday afternoon, and the whole of my time since then has been consumed, literally *consumed*, I assure you, with trying to find out what on earth this sorry debacle is all about. Indeed, I find it a matter of some regret that this matter went outside the School before I could be apprised of it, and could probably have hushed it up and spared us all the pain of this meeting, as well as whatever else is to come."

At this he lifted his head and gave a rare glance in Lorraine's direction over the top of his spectacles.

"Poor Yunus," said a female voice originating from somewhere inside a baggy t-shirt but outside his eye line. Matthews lifted a genial, pacifying hand in its direction.

"However," he continued, "Lorraine has revealed the official policy on this sort of thing to me and I accept that it was probably incumbent upon her to make a snap decision and we shall all just have to live with the consequences of that snap decision. It seems that Yunus did have what they call a 'terrorist document' on his office computer, and his story is that he was sent it by a student with whom he is friendly in the School of Politics, because that student had asked him to print it out for free on account of the fact that he, the Politics student, didn't want to pay for the printing himself. But it was apparently all *bona fide*, the document was genuinely for the student's research. We can probably all be generous enough to overlook the low-level dishonesty in the arrangement. I know I am minded to. No point in rocking the boat for a few quid's worth of paper and toner, slap on the wrist kind of thing for Yunus, eh, softly softly? Or so I thought. In fact, I went straight over to the Registrar's office first thing this morning with the intention, quite frankly, of giving him a kick in the wind and demanding that he put an end to all this palaver and stop playing it all so by-the-book, not least because we are missing the sterling services of our young administrator and are all having to do things ourselves that we don't know how to do but he did. We all know that he cannot exactly be replaced by a temp, now, can he? But I'm afraid that that's when things got a bit more complicated. What I am about to say should remain in this room, but the problem for us is not simply that our Yunus has been, I must say I think rather ludicrously, arrested under the Terrorism Act, but we have a much bigger problem in that there is now apparently some, er, confusion as to his immigration status. It seems, although Yunus has been with us for about eleven months, that no one has yet definitively checked his right to work in the country. So the much bigger problem that faces us now is that we are likely to be without an assistant School administrator for quite some time."

At this there were groans.

Matthews looked again at Lorraine.

"It's not my responsibility to check his immigration status," Lorraine said defensively but firmly. "That's an HR function. Indeed, I spent months reminding them of it and eventually gave up."

"Och, but wait a minute here!" exclaimed a Caledonian voice from the row of staff opposite, among whom Redman sat. Redman did not bother to pitch forward and look. He knew that the voice belonged to Dr Donald Doyle – the School's very own The Donald – who had succeeded him as Union secretary when Redman had resigned the previous term. This ascension to office, as well as the fact that this year of 2017 was the centenary of the event that he considered the high point of all history, had got Doyle's considerable dander up even more than usual. The Donald was an aggressive Trotskyite with Chinese teeth and a scar across his small hard slit of a mouth which he attempted to disguise with a ragged red beard and an unkempt moustache. McNamara had once told Redman that Doyle hailed from Shettleston, a much rougher part of Glasgow even than McNamara's, "lumpenproletarian as compared to ordinary proletarian" was how McNamara had put it, and that this would largely explain Doyle's instinctive bluntness, his inflexible ideology-controlled thinking, and his simple-minded politics.

"Jist wait a minute," Doyle went on. "Noo look here, Bernie, yae huv tae be kiddin' us, right? The real issue here isnae the lad's papers. Ah think we aw know that's a complete red herrin'. If Ah've ever seen an *ex post facto*, that's wan. Thuv gone lookin' fur that oan purpose tae spare thur blushes. The polis, Ah mean, mebbe University management anaw. The cops know the kid's no' a terrorist an' that whit they did wis jist racial profilin', pure an' simple. Nae way, absolutely nae way, wid the boys ha' bin clapped in irons if they wur white, um Ah right?"

There were murmurs of assent from a few people around the table who had managed to understand fully what Doyle was saying in his broad uncompromising patois. Redman felt his eyes wander in irritated boredom around the room, eventually alighting on Sergei Krokoff, who was secretly reading a book, as he often did in staff meetings, especially during Doyle's dogmatic and hectoring monologues, of which the Ukrainian freely confessed he had never understood a word. Poor Krokoff, Redman reflected ruefully, the abject he of the Jane Blake Public Interest Disclosure document which Nigel Asterisk had given to Redman the previous November and which Redman had felt obliged, because the older man was mentioned in it, to pass to McNamara, as well as to force Asterisk to suppress. Krokoff, the sorry dupe. Krokoff was out of it, this was all happening in a different world to his, one that did not concern Krokoff in the remotest fashion. And yet Redman envied Krokoff a little in that moment. Nothing whatsoever trespassed on his insouciance, for sure.

Doyle had meanwhile been droning on. "Naw, whit we huv here is a wrangful arrest uv wan ae oor number, uv an ordinary worker, in fact, made under completely reactionary legislation, an' that's the real thing up fur discussion. An' whit we need noo is solidarity, no' jist blubberin' ower the fact thit we'll aw huv tae dae mair a' oor ain admin. Wuv goat tae stawn up an' be coontit, ev'ry wan ae us. Illegal immigrant ma erse. Naebiddy roon this table cared if he wis illegal or no' 'til noo. Kid's a total scapegoat. An' let's no' furget, there's another scapegoat tae, the other wee yin, the student fae Politics, whit's his name, Faraj? Ah wisnae in the buildin' it the time, but those a' ye that wur aw saw him wrangfully arrested right here in oor corridor oan Monday efternin. Thur hooses huv bin raided and thur bein' illegally detained. Noo, the Union executive's discussed this, it its lunchtime meetin' the day, an' there's a plan uv action developin', so Ah say we haud oan an' wait for their cue. It'll come soon enough. Untae then, let's make sure we don't keep quiet aboot it at aw, in fact, but *tell everbiddy* whit happened here and start drummin' up support fur these two innocent lads. This could be big. It's already aw oor the papers."

There was a brief silence, except for one or two indefinite *uh-huhs*. In the chair, Matthews, who also found Doyle tricky to understand and frankly rather intimidating, hesitated a considerable few seconds before summoning himself to respond, but as he did so he was spared by Redman, who said, with a great definiteness that Matthews found rather impressive, and again without moving forward to look at Doyle, "No."

Lorraine exchanged stares with him across the room.

"Whit?" Doyle roused himself and lurched forward to squint along the row of seats at Redman in the corner. "*Whit?*"

All eyes turned on Redman.

"No," he said. "Hardly any of that is true. It's not at all the case, for example, that his immigration status is irrelevant. It's extremely relevant and cannot be ignored. Granted, that was not why he was arrested but, if one potential offence comes to light in the investigation of another, it's hardly surprising or unusual. And we simply cannot say that we don't care about employment law. We all should care about employment law. It's there to protect us in our jobs. But most of all, neither of these arrests was wrongful and nobody is being illegally detained. I don't personally approve of the provisions of the Prevention of

Terrorism Act, but if you've looked at it, you'll see that it provides for arrest on the grounds of mere possession of a so-called 'terrorist document', which it appears is incontrovertibly true in the case of both of these suspects. So the arrests were perfectly legal and not in the slightest wrongful. That is, they were in complete accordance with the law governing arrest and the law under which they were arrested. The Act permits detention for up to twenty-eight days without charge, but charges can be brought only if, in addition to possession, it appears that the possession was with a view actually to committing an act of terrorism. That does seem far too long a time to me, but that's the law, and only two days have so far passed. The police are entitled to take longer to establish the facts. There is no particular reason why we should accept the story given by the suspects, though it may turn out to be true. We simply don't know enough to rush to judgment or action. And lastly, this has absolutely nothing to do with the Union. Neither of these two men were UCU members or eligible for membership."

This was all said in a steady voice, but by half way through it Doyle's slightly demented eyes were already darting in their sockets and, by the end of it, his lower jaw was hanging in a satirical, somewhat malicious grin, as if he were enjoying in advance the put-down with which he intended to rebut.

"Ye done?" he jabbed at Redman. "Bugger the law. It's an unjust law. An' you urnae a UCU member either any mair, so don't tell those of us who ur whit's the Union's business and whit isnae."

Redman sighed deeply. He felt a blow-up coming on.

*

63

At the same moment, in the common room of the School of Politics, McNamara was likewise immured in a staff meeting, witnessing with almost complete detachment a now fully developed verbal blow-up in its violent, ongoing eruption. It was not simply that he refused to engage in the openly confrontational discourse that had come quickly to define the meeting. In fact, he was more akin to Sergei Krokoff than to Redman, at least in that, though he did understand what was actually being said, he did not appreciate why any of the participants seemed to care so passionately about it. In the scheme of things, in McNamara's mind, it all seemed piteously trivial. His mind was more occupied with what he considered truly important things.

By contrast with the ongoing exchange in the School of English, here the antlers currently locked were right-wing rather than left-wing. In the chair was Professor Frank Dashwood, a distinguished conservative political scientist who was currently a minor consultant to a Whitehall think-tank advising Theresa May's government on its Brexit plans. For ten minutes he had been parrying increasingly intense onrushes of censure, castigation and contumely from Bradley Gooltree, the doctoral supervisor of the arrested student, who had once been in the military and knew nothing at all about politics, yet had managed to secure a job at Odium to teach about the trendy grant-attracting topic of terrorism, of which he had certainly experienced something, but on which he now adopted a pragmatic liberal stance rather than the bellicose waterboard-all-jihadi-bastards line he knew he had advocated, and indeed put into practice a few times, while on active service as a sergeant in the Parachute Regiment.

Occasionally Dashwood would look over at McNamara as if soliciting his aid. The two men had, over the years, built a fairly solid bridge, of mutual respect if not friendship, that spanned the ideological gulf between them, at least on the purely personal level. McNamara found Dashwood to be competent, honest, hard-working, decent, well balanced, and of good humour, with admittedly the major personality *hamartia* of being a dreadful reactionary. Dashwood considered McNamara's politics to be other-planetary, but undogmatic, just as the man himself seemed well-rounded, worldly-wise, tolerant, phlegmatic, knowledgeable and humane. He had met with McNamara before the meeting and asked him, without guile, if he would offer his assistance should things get as hot-under-the-collar as he expected them to. McNamara had seemed sincerely puzzled at the idea that there might be any trouble at all and mumbled words to the effect that he was sure Dashwood could deal with it if it arose. Now that daggers were being openly drawn, Dashwood was hoping that McNamara would intervene, and was beginning to feel uncomfortably under pressure and isolated. No one seemed to be on his side or prepared to defend him in what he knew was his perfectly rational response to the situation, and moreover one which he had no other choice but to make, given the advice he had already sought from, or rather been given by, senior management. There was, Dashwood knew, a great deal of personal vindictiveness abroad in the room, because every member of the School's academic staff except him had voted for Britain to remain in the EU, and some of them, particularly a small trio of conspiratorial Germans whom he and McNamara privately called the Red Army

Faction, feared for the long-term security of their jobs. Anything that might increase the heat below this already simmering pot of personal animus was likely to be fed into the fire.

"I tell you again," Gooltree was saying emphatically, "I spoke to the police for *three whole hours* yesterday and I told them Faraj was a genuine postgraduate student and that this document was a legitimate document for him to possess for the purposes of academic research and that they had absolutely no reason to hold him in custody. But they just wouldn't listen. They kept asking me all kinds of irrelevant stuff about his behaviour and his friends and his political views, things that are personally intrusive and impertinent and off the point. Even when I told them I used to be in the Paras and I was on their side and I was no radical, they just would not yield. I wrote to the Registrar and the Vice Chancellor yesterday evening expressing my outrage at the whole thing but I have yet to get a response. So what I want you to do as Head of School is stop stonewalling, stop thinking just about your own position, and get down there and give this new VC a good talking-to and make him exert his influence to get *this innocent student of ours* out of jail."

Dashwood had been struggling to get in a word. He now was permitted a reply. "I heard you the first time you said all that, Brad, but you didn't answer my question. Did you *know* he was going to download this document? Did he tell you he was? Because it might make a significant difference if he did and if you then advised him of the legal issues involved. But if he didn't, why didn't he? And it looks as if he didn't because there has been no prior communication from us notifying him that it was acceptable to do so."

Gooltree's entire upper body, and indeed his legs below the desk, shook in tremors of exasperation throughout Dashwood's speech, but still he did not answer.

"Vy? For vot reason?" This was from a member of the Red Army Faction, Griselda Rotfang, also known to Dashwood as Ulrike Meinhoff, a blubbery-jowled scowl atop a flak jacket at the back of the room. "Vy should he do zat, seek anyvone's permission? He is adult, is ziss not so? He is doing ze research. Vot does he need ze permission for? Zis is a democracy, zer is ze freedom, zer is no censorship, he is arrested for nussing."

"Well," said Dashwood patiently, "there is the very small obstruction of the Prevention of Terrorism Act. I believe they have a similar thing in Germany, Griselda, no? And there is the even tinier but still significant problem of the University's general and our own School's particular code governing the ethics of research procedures, the latter enforced by a standing committee in the School, on which Brad here *happens actually to sit*, and which approves or rejects detailed formal applications and otherwise advises students on the ethics of potentially controversial research actions with a view to compliance and record, one of which such actions rather obviously happens to be obtaining an ISIS training manual that gives instructions on and advocates murdering innocent people, but which this student seems to have just gone ahead and downloaded on a School computer off his own bat and then sent through the University email system to a member of staff in another School. If we could show that we approved this action in advance then the outlook would be rather rosier for the student. But from the police's point of view the fact that we knew damn all about it looks potentially incriminating for him, as if the student seems deliberately to have concealed the action from us in a manner *not entirely disconsonant* with what an actual terrorist might do in order to prevent detection."

Dashwood glanced again imploringly at McNamara. But McNamara was there in body only. His thoughts were in fact dwelling, as they still did every day, on the mystery that was Cannon Buckrack, a man he had never met or even seen, whose mere voice he had heard on a recording of just one short telephone call, someone of whom he knew nothing other than the four syllables of his name, but who had for some unaccountable reason chosen him, Robert McNamara, to be the recipient of communications which had led to and explained the dramatic downfall of Sir Evan Covet, the seemingly irrepressible Vice Chancellor of the University of Odium until only three months before. Then he thought of Jane Blake's Public Interest Disclosure submission, a copy of which he had been given by Redman while both she and Covet were already freezing side-by-side in the same police mortuary, the one that had outlined Covet's plan to have her seduce McNamara, to entrap him into disgrace, for what? For his politics? According to Jane's document, her purpose as a tutor in the student hall of residence McNamara oversaw had really been to implement Covet's malicious design upon him. She was a sexual weapon in a proxy personal war that McNamara had not known was even being waged, and his sense of violation at the time this knowledge came to him had shaken him deeply. And yet he could not consciously recall a single occasion on which the young woman had said or done anything remotely suggestive or flirtatious or ambiguous in his presence. In his remembrance she had been entirely chaste. Had he simply not noticed? Was he really so enamoured of Rachel Brace at the time that he had entirely missed the erotic overtures of such a beautiful young woman? Jane herself had claimed in writing that she had made such attempts on his person. But she had later also sent a written withdrawal of that document. Had she made it up just to blackmail Covet, who seemed to have paid her off the very night she retracted it? Did anyone have the answers to these questions? Was he ever to have them settled?

He became eventually aware of loudening voices in the meeting and he looked up and saw Dashwood struggling, beleaguered, put through the wringer, perspiring, barely holding his own.

"Yes!" exclaimed someone loudly, emphatically, a note of zestful self-righteousness in the male voice. "Vot about ze *academic freedom*, huh?"

McNamara raised his hand to catch Dashwood's attention. Dashwood saw it as a benediction and returned a beseeching look, feeling that a silent prayer had at last been acknowledged.

"I shall speak now," McNamara said. He turned in the direction of the last utterance, knowing precisely whose it was. He faced the lanky, blond Dr Heinz Benz, the Andreas Baader of the Teutons, so tall his legs sprawled several feet out below the deskline, his entire body so sketchy and stick-like that it gave the appearance of a geometrician's teaching accessory, seeming to be capable of up to fifty-seven varieties of angle in any single posture.

"Do students," McNamara enquired, with apparent naïvety, "have academic freedom?"

Benz paused to think for a moment then nodded efficiently. "Yes, of course, zey should have ze academic freedom."

"No," said McNamara politely. "I was not asking for a normative, but rather a constative, answer."

Benz paused again for exactly the same amount of time and once more his head oscillated with the same precision engineering. "Yes, of course, zey should have ze academic freedom."

"I shall try once more, Heinz," McNamara persevered. "Are you expressing a *wish* that they *should* have academic freedom or do you think it a *fact* that they already *do* enjoy this freedom?"

Various algorithms ran rapidly within Benz's software and came up with a query which sounded, because speech has no question marks, like a paradox. "Zey have zis freedom, zey do not?"

McNamara sat back in order to draw his catechism to a close. "They do not. This is a plain matter of statute, both Parliamentary and University. The Parliamentary statute ensures academic freedom for the institution. That is, it guarantees the non-interference of the state in the University's freedom to teach and research on what it chooses. Anyone who knows, to take an example entirely at random, German history of the 'thirties and 'forties, will understand the supreme value of such formalised legal protection. The University statute guarantees a similar freedom to teach and research, even on controversial subjects, without threat to one's employment, as long as one's activity is within the law, *for its academic staff*. But not for its students. No question of academic freedom in the matter of these two arrests, therefore, can possibly arise."

Benz recovered quickly from the brief does-not-compute expression which flickered across his face. "Ah, no, ze usser arrested man, ze one ze student sent ze file to, he was a member of ze staff, so –"

"He was a member of the *administrative* staff," McNamara specified, "not of the *academic* staff. Thus neither of the two arrested men can claim that their academic freedom was breached, because neither of them has academic freedom. It is most important that you understand this, so that you do not go off at a misleading and quite untrue tangent. Now that you do know it, to argue that either of these men has academic freedom would be an act of wilful demagoguery."

A few swift internal sub-routines later, Benz, his CPU evidently a little under strain, mustered the fragile reply, "Zen I zink zat is outrageous. Ze students should have zis freedom."

"It's a matter of established law who has the freedom and who doesn't," said McNamara.

Griselda Rotfang, adopting a pose of ostentatious comradeship, like a Dorothy showing sympathy beside the suddenly dented Tin Man of Heinz Benz, summoned up a dark grimace of uglier-than-usual power. "Zen zis is a wrong law. Zis is an unequal law. I say *fick* and *scheiße* and *verpiss dich* to zis law!"

McNamara sighed deeply. He felt a meltdown coming on.

Chapter Five

McNamara exited his father's house and turned right into Northgate Road. After a few minutes a road-sweeping vehicle approached on the far side and then suddenly stopped. He could see the driver, though in silhouette only, twisting round and looking deliberately towards him. He walked away, ignoringly.

The scene changed. He was now half a mile further on, striding purposefully past what had been his aunt's house on Wallacewell Road. A lorry was coming towards him. The road-sweeper appeared once more, this time on the wrong side of the road, driving towards the truck. Again it stopped, this time veering so that other vehicle had to brake and mount the pavement. As he drew level with it, McNamara looked into the cabin. There was a much younger man than him in there, with blond punky hair and a nose ring, looking out at him, clearly waiting for him.

The other truck was now suddenly not there at all. Looking through the window, McNamara had a sense of watching TV with the sound down. The younger man was talking to him, addressing questions to him which McNamara lip-read as, "You don't remember me?" and

"You've decided to stop and talk at last?"

McNamara went up close to the side of the cabin and shielded his eyes from the sunlight in order to see better. With the window still closed, he asked to whom he was speaking. The young man simply sneered and mouthed, "Look at this." Then he turned his head all the way around. The bottom half of it was shaven clean, with the blond hair shooting out only above the earline. Below this line was a tattoo of a map of a somewhat misshapen England and Wales. There was no Scotland, or, if there were, it was hidden underneath the hair

McNamara pulled open the door, seized the stranger by the back of the collar and dragged him out onto the pavement, demanding to know who he was and what business he had with him. The young man repeated phrases which were still only lip movements with no sound and which, although the words varied, all had the same gist: "Oh, you still don't know..."

Again the scene dissolved and resolved. They were not any longer in the road, but in the dark shell of McNamara's bombed-out bedroom on Petershill Drive, yet another mile further down a familiar route. The heavier McNamara had the stranger pinned against the wall and was threatening him with violence if he did not explain himself. The other offered no resistance at all, seemed limp and acquiescent, and it now occurred to McNamara that maybe this was some kind of trap into which he had been cleverly lured. He had the sense that the young man's hands, which were clasped at the back of McNamara's waist, were moving, manipulating. Then he felt something plunge into the small of his back with a sharp sting. A needle, perhaps. The arms around him suddenly formed into a tighter grip, and McNamara surmised that he was being drugged. He felt himself slipping out of consciousness, and at that moment the stranger began to laugh obscenely, to roll his tongue around his lips, and then he leaned in close, and began to lick McNamara's face...

When McNamara reared up from the bed, Redman's diminutive Jack Russell was toppled back on his haunches and seemed alarmed for a moment, though by some gymnastic miracle he reached the floor on all fours and began energetically to chase his tail. With a start, and just managing to stifle a petrified moan, McNamara saw a slim figure in dark cameo in the frame of the bedroom doorway.

"Only me, Robert," said Redman.

McNamara felt the shock recede, then his heart began to race. "What the fuck, James?"

"You forget?" asked Redman. "I told you we were running in this morning and you agreed to dogsit. You said you'd leave the back door open."

McNamara groaned as he remembered. "Christ, I don't know what smells worse, your dog's breath or your BO."

"Never mind us," Redman replied. "What is the bloody stink *in here*?" He had crossed to the desk by the bed and was now pointing at the smoking paraphernalia strewn atop it – a pouch of light Golden Virginia, a nearly empty packet of Rizlas, a small and not empty baggie, an ashtray. "Jesus, Robert, I thought you handed all the dope you confiscate over to security?"

McNamara rubbed his eyes with his hands and grumbled, "Well, I have a new policy now. I destroy it myself. I burn it."

"Bit of a risk, no?" Redman cautioned.

"What risk? At my age? I'm nearly sixty. You think I

need this job anymore? You think I care about any of it?"

"Still, there'd be the embarrassment, no?"

"Fuck embarrassment," McNamara growled. "Christ, it's legal in half of America these days. This country is beginning to feel like it's in its own Prohibition era."

"Eeeeew!" Redman suddenly exclaimed with disgust. "What the fuck is *this*?"

He was pointing at the iPad on the desk.

McNamara sagged and fell back on the pillow and let his eyelids flutter shut. "Did something happen to you in childhood, James? How did you never develop a sense of privacy? So what, I watched some porno and jacked off. It helps me sleep. Don't tell me you don't do that."

"Well, yeah," said Redman, "but I don't shoot my load *all over the screen*!"

"Don't worry, it's waterproof, wipe clean. Tell you what, why not offer it to that maniac pipsqueak hound of yours? He'll probably lap it up."

"Euch!" Redman exploded, and bent down to the dog and ruffled his ears and babytalked him. "Don't you listen to the nasty man! Don't you pay any heed to Professor McNamara! I won't let him poison you with his penis juice!" Then, still crouching, he laughed and said to McNamara, "Good to know your engine still goes, though, I suppose."

McNamara sighed.

"Will you, please," he said with exaggerated tolerance, "fuck off downstairs and make some coffee, and take that neurotic cur with you? When I said I'd leave the door open I was not imagining you would free-roam about my house like a Puritan prosecutor,

75

feeling licensed to pass comment on my drug habits and levels of cock energy! Do you have a search warrant? No, thought not. So bugger off out of my bedroom. I will join you in five minutes once I have washed this sandpaper tongue-scum off my face."

Redman retreated to the kitchen and, in due course, McNamara padded downstairs to join him.

"So check this out," said Redman, pulling an iPad mini from his rucksack. He flipped it open and added jocularly, "You won't mind if we use my iPad rather than yours?"

McNamara reached for his glasses.

"They already have a Facebook group," Redman continued. "Links to newspaper and TV coverage, links to half-baked blogosphere coverage, they've even got a legal fund going this early, there are sweet mini-hagiographies of Yunus and Faraj. Apparently they are 'human rights activists' now. They've been leading a secret political life, it would seem. Faraj has had a little underground political mag going for the past year, apparently, some kind of insipid Chomsky-inspired libertarian left-leaning online thing, to which Yunus is a regular contributor. Needless to say, no mention of the other kinds of contributions Faraj squirts into his Yunus. Innocent and idealistic youngsters in every way, it would appear. The Odium Two, they're being called."

"What?" McNamara was incredulous. "By analogy with the Birmingham Six, say? That's laughable. The two of them haven't even been charged, never mind convicted. But who is 'they'? I mean, who has set up the Facebook groups? Yunus and Faraj are still in detention, it's only three days in, they'll get to speak with no one, so they can't have done it."

"Nominally," said Redman, "it's our very own Ivy

Littletot, Students' Union president. She's the official Facebook group owner, at least. She'll be all fired up after her crusade last term, no doubt, except apparently she does not have the favour of the new VC the way she had with Covet, and so this time she's not defending senior management but attacking it. However, my suspicion is that the whole thing is the brainchild of Donald Doyle, probably with Avril Poon's connivance. They can't act formally as the two most senior Union officers because it's not strictly speaking a Union matter and hard to make into one, and they probably don't want to risk losing a vote at a Union general meeting so early, so my guess is that they're turning it into an unofficial campaign instead, looking to build a groundswell of popular support, which they'll then use as a fulcrum to get the Union formally involved. Just look at the press coverage – it's gone international in just three days. I mean, yesterday's *Le Monde*, for godsake? The media to Poon is like dung to a beetle. She's bound to be right at the centre of this."

McNamara held the small screen closer and intoned from the list of news outlets. "BBC, ITN, Channel 4, every broadsheet except the *Telegraph*, the *International Herald Tribune*, the – what? – the *Taipei Times*? Why is it being reported in Taiwan, of all places?"

"Reuters," Redman shrugged. "They syndicated it."

McNamara had clicked on one of the links. "Yes, I see. But this *Le Monde* piece, it's all wrong, it refers to them as 'un professeur et un étudiant'."

"Because that's what Reuters syndicated. When you refer to 'a member of staff' in a university the usual assumption is that you mean an academic. So keep it ambiguous, like that, in your press release, and watch the media make the assumption you hope they will, is my guess as to what they did."

"Christ!" McNamara burst out. "This local group has over a thousand members already! In three days?"

"All they have to do," said McNamara, "is click 'join group'. But what's more important is that it also has over four thousand shares."

"What does that mean?"

"Over four thousand members have posted it on their own Facebook timelines. That takes just two clicks. Remember, this group was set up only yesterday morning. Some of our students have hundreds and even thousands of Facebook friends. The group is going viral. The next thing we'll probably see is that that exponential sharing in itself becomes a media story. The whole trick, which Poon knows well, is to keep new things happening so that coverage can be ongoing."

"Look at all these comments," McNamara said. "They go on forever. Christ, academic freedom! Pffft. It's all rumour and gossip and assertion and exaggerated speculation. It's close to fantasy. These people know nothing at all."

Redman nodded. "But it's a snowball running downhill. Keep liking and sharing and commenting and it soon becomes unignorable. It signifies by its mere ubiquity. It must be true because so many people can't be wrong. McLuhan was a bit premature, but what he said is true now: the medium really is the message."

"Yes, but come on, it's a storm in a teacup. They'll be let out soon. I don't think these two are terrorists, do you?"

"Of course not," Redman agreed. "But if I were the police, I'm not so sure I'd let them go so quickly. For one thing, the police will see it differently from us.

They'll want to comb through everything, and they'll want to throw up some mud to make the arrests seem reasonable. I assume that's what the kerfuffle about Yunus's immigration status is all about."

"What is he?" asked McNamara. "Moroccan?"

"Tunisian," said Redman. "So, remember the Tunisian beach attack two years back? Thirty of the thirty-eight murdered were British. There's a big fat flag in Tunisia on their terrorist maps."

"But Faraj is a Brit, right?"

"Yeah, he's an Odium kid, lives with his family in the east end. Apparently the cops have turned their house upside down. I think they'll keep the two of them a little while longer and then they'll release Faraj but hold on to Yunus on an illegal immigration charge."

"Then that should cripple the campaign, no? I mean, illegal immigration, that's peanuts compared to terrorism. You can't build a mass campaign around a single dodgy passport. And remember, this is Odium, hardly a centre of student protest. Stick him on a plane back to Tunis. End of."

"You think?" said Redman. "I'm not so sure. I have a feeling about Faraj. He's an expert needler, he likes to provoke, he's got sharp little chips on both shoulders. He's an attention-seeker. He was virtually asking to be arrested in the corridor the other day. I can't see him walking free and just settling back down into a seat in the University library to tap out the next chapter of his Ph.D., especially if his lover is still in detention. He likes the drama. He's an *activist*. He'll be intoxicated by the minor celebrity. He'll be the poster boy for what he will think of as a mass movement, inside this little goldfish bowl at any rate. Just imagine the next number of his webzine. All this material! And you haven't forgotten, have you, that Trump is coming? This is surely all going to be repackaged and delivered anew during his visit."

McNamara was surprised. "Trump? Coming here? Since when?"

"You didn't see Spooner's press statement on the news on Monday?"

"I don't follow all that shit. I mean, who cares? What's he coming for?"

"I'm putting your slow thinking down to the smokety-smokes you've been having, Robert," Redman replied. "Obviously, he's coming to hand over the cheque, in two weeks. He's apparently coming to Odium right off Airforce One, even before he goes down to Number Ten. It's just possible that Theresa May might have to show up here at the same time in order not to appear slighted. Now just imagine that, a mere three weeks after all this. Trump the pussy-grabbing racist, May the right-wing isolationist, both descending from the skies above Odium at the same time? You bet they are going to keep this campaign rolling and tie it into that."

McNamara shook his head in comic despair. "I see. That will provide a focus for all kinds of high jinks," he agreed.

Redman picked up his iPad and shook it. "If only this were all," he said, putting it in his bag and removing a couple of stapled sheets of paper. "But there are also suddenly very virulent and *engaged* collective emails, in my School anyway, flying in all directions from students whose idea until yesterday of a political novel was something like Ian McEwan's *Saturday*. And then there's this, which I got last evening."

He handed over the pages, and slowly drank his

coffee while McNamara perused it.

PRESS RELEASE
22 February 2017

Odium University Staff and Students Protest Against the Use of the Terrorism Act on Campus and Demand Academic Freedom

Two members of the University of Odium, one a student and one staff, were arrested on Monday, 20 February. Concerned students and staff wish to express concerns about the operation on a number of grounds.

1. Academic freedom
The arrests purport to be in connection with "radical material", which the student did possess, but only for research purposes. Lecturers in his department, as well as academics elsewhere in the University, are deeply perturbed by the ramifications of his arrest for academia and political research. An academic who knows the arrested student well explained that his research focused on contemporary political issues which are highly pertinent to current foreign policy. The criminalisation of research of this nature undermines academic freedom, suggesting serious political constraints on what may be researched at a university.

2. Racism and Islamophobia
There is universal agreement that the arrests would not have occurred had the two men been white. The zealous nature of the operation, which caused great

distress to the men, was encouraged by their ethnicity and religious backgrounds. Police conduct during the operation, including the targeting of other ethnic minority students for questioning, also suggests institutional racism. When the arrests are looked at in relation to heightened "security" measures, official harassment of Muslims, and widespread withdrawal of civil liberties, a picture of a damaging climate created by terrorism legislation becomes evident.

3. Use of Terrorism Act to attack political activists

While questioning members of the University who had not been arrested, the police have been collating information on student activism and peaceful campaigns. They asked many questions about the student peace magazine "Resolution", for which both arrested men write, and about other political student activities. The presence of the police on campus has fomented fear amongst some students. Many see the operation as a warning from the police that they are likely to arrest anyone engaged in peaceful political activities.

4. Behaviour of the University

The University's near-complete silence on the matter has upset students and academics. Its one short statement (published on Tuesday, 21 February) constituted nothing more than a request that students, however they react to the arrests, should not "unsettle the peace of the campus". Meanwhile, the University appears to have called the police onto campus in large numbers to ensure that students and academics initiate no organised political action. The University has ignored the fear caused by the large police presence and investigation into legitimate political activities, the concern of staff and students about the criminalisation of research, the racist and Islamophobic nature of the police's conduct, and the signs that the University provided information to the police on its own members, potentially racially profiling its staff and students.

Academics and students throughout the University of Odium, and members of the public from the wider community, are demanding:

a. The right to academic freedom;
b. An end to the criminalisation of political research;
c. A stop to police and University racism and Islamophobia and the full enjoyment of civil rights and liberties.

We demand that the University of Odium publicly:

a. Acknowledges the disturbing nature of the police response, and makes a formal complaint to the police;
b. Admits the unreserved innocence of the student and staff members arrested;
c. Apologises for the distress caused to them, their families, and their friends;
d. Guarantees academic and political freedom;
e. Commits itself to freedom of speech and freedom of expression on campus.

[ENDS]

Notes for editors:

The document above will be published in the form of a petition in the next week, to be signed by professors, lecturers, other University staff, students, and members of the wider community. An ongoing campaign will be organised against the improper use of terrorism legislation, along with lawyers, academics, students, and members of the public.

McNamara removed his spectacles. "I'd call it sub-hysterical. It almost constantly draws attention to its own tendentiousness. It jumps to conclusions like a lemming, wilfully interpreting simple facts in the most paranoid manner conceivable. It uses intemperate motivating adjectives in excess. It's amateur demagoguery of the most obvious kind, a discourse of smoke and mirrors aimed at producing the cheapest polemical effects. 'There is universal agreement that the arrests would not have occurred had the two men been white.' That's just transparent bunk, it's simply made up to incite, it's based on no evidence of general opinion at all. And the entire document deliberately omits to mention the key fact that the 'member of staff' was not an academic in order to disguise the bankruptcy of what it has to say about academic freedom. As for the demands, well, they're beyond preposterous. No one is stopping anyone doing any kind of political research. We can do whatever we damn well want. We can even download ISIS training manuals if we like, we just have to clear it first,

84

obviously, and leave a paper trail of the approval, but that would be a formality. This fool of a student just decided to ignore that elementary procedure. Still, who'd have thought, eh, the University of Odium and politics? Oil and water can mix after all." He tossed the papers on the kitchen table with distaste. "But that! It's written with such political bombast, as if the authors had waited all their lives to pen something in the nature of a radical manifesto, and were gagging on their own narcissism all the while that they did so. Who would you say is responsible?"

Redman smiled wryly. "It's Doyle translated by Poon, for my money. Though it looks as if Gooltree gave them a quote."

"Gooltree!" McNamara's head flapped from side to side again. "The vile cunt used to shoot Muslims dead for a living. I wonder how many he helped to rendition or pack off to Guantanamo."

"Perhaps," Redman ventured, "he experienced a conversion on the road to Damascus."

McNamara laughed wearily. "James, are you laying these things before me the way the Devil offered Jesus all the kingdoms of the world while he was in the wilderness? Because I see no kingdoms of the world here. I do get the sense, however, that you want to *do* something."

Redman regarded him for a moment. "No," he said, "but I am intending to accept Spooner's offer of the Vice Deanship of Arts when we see him tomorrow. And that is going to inveigle me into the Trump scenario."

"You are?" McNamara could hardly disguise his astonishment. "Well, good luck with that."

"You see," Redman explained, "it will frankly give me some say, some power even. I can go on sitting where I am, seeing things from the perspective of a lowly frog, or I can accept the opportunity to help direct things. Why risk letting someone else get that kind of control? We know there are very few who won't bungle it. I also wouldn't mind three years away from teaching, to be candid. But if I am going to accept it, and my reading of the runes is correct, I am going to have to ride a big bucking contradiction. So how all this plays out is something that concerns me vitally."

McNamara nodded. "I understand. I really do."

"And you?" Redman rejoined. "You won't consider the Deanship of Social Sciences?"

McNamara shook his head.

"So," Redman said, "you won't be coming to the meeting with Spooner tomorrow?"

McNamara seemed to consider gravely for a moment.

"Actually," he said with thought, "I think I shall."

Chapter Six

After showering and changing at McNamara's, Redman walked up the hill to the Trump Building. It was only nine-fifteen and the School of English was quiet. He tapped on Lorraine's office door and turned the handle and was surprised to find it locked. He took out his mobile and called hers and heard it ringing inside the office. She answered.

"It's me," he said. "I'm outside in the corridor."

"Oh," she said. "Wait."

A minute later the door was unlocked and she opened it. He could see that her eyes were red with tears.

"Come in," she said, and locked the door again behind him. She stepped towards him, asking for his arms to encircle her. He took her to him and held her warmly.

"What's wrong?" he asked into her ear.

"It's today's *Guardian*," she said. "It's on the table there. It names me as the person who reported on Yunus and even has a picture of me from the University website. It also has a quote from Matthews saying he knew nothing about it. But they didn't call me up for a quote. I got no chance to comment. And now other papers are ringing. *The Daily Mail*, for godsake, though they actually seemed sympathetic. *The Times*. I just said no comment and hung up. And now the hate mail has started arriving. Emails from anonymous addresses, things on Facebook from fake identities, even those two things there, I found them slipped under the door when I arrived. Don't read them, they're vile."

Disobeying her, Redman picked up the two notes, took them in, and blanched. Next he looked at *The Guardian*, already open at the appropriate page. By the time he had finished he was seething with repressed rage.

"When did this thing become such a snot rag?" he said rhetorically. Then, to her: "You should go home. This is just the beginning."

"But Matthews –"

"I'll go and talk to Matthews. But you shouldn't have to put up with this. This is a justifiable reason for absence. In fact, if you're not here, Matthews is likely to feel a greater sense of crisis – no you, no Yunus, he'll start to sense that things are falling apart in the School. So go. Let me have these."

He picked up the hate notes and *The Guardian*.

"Alright," she said. "Will you come over tonight?"

"I'll come over before tonight."

He put his hand behind her head and drew her to him for a short kiss.

She smiled. "I love you."

He kissed her again, longer this time, saying, "And I love you. Now let me go and talk to Matthews and don't be here when I come back."

When he knocked on Matthews' door he did not wait to be invited in, but entered without ceremony.

The top half of Matthews' face was visible above his computer screen, the back of which faced the door.

"Oh, hello, James," Matthews said. "Can it wait?"

"No, I'm afraid not." Redman brandished *The Guardian*. "Have you seen this?"

"Er, no, I don't –"

"Quote: 'Professor Matthews said that Ms Quant had reported the matter to senior management without either his permission or authority.' Unquote."

"Oh," said Matthews. "Good. I'm glad they quoted me correctly. Bothersome business, this."

"Bothersome? It's certainly bothering Lorraine. She's had hate mail, you want to see?"

He put the notes in front of Matthews, who peered at them silently.

"Blimey," said Matthews. "A bit harsh."

"A bit *harsh*? She's got emails and Facebook messages as well. Other newspapers are calling her up. She's had to go home. She's shocked and depressed and feels hurt and threatened."

"Oh, dear God, no!" Matthews expostulated. "She's gone off sick? I've got to finish this Everyman edition of *England, My England* by the end of the month. Now's not the time."

"Has it occurred to you, Bernard, that you should be defending your staff, not hanging them out to dry?"

"But I don't know what you mean," said Matthews defensively. "I am defending the staff. I'm supporting Yunus. He's in jail, you know."

Redman heard his voice rising in volume. "He's in jail because he had an ISIS training manual on his PC! Lorraine has done nothing questionable at all. She followed procedure!"

"Yes, yes, of course, I know," Matthews said. "I didn't mean I was supporting Yunus *against* her."

"Well, that's what it looks like from this!"

"Really?" said Matthews. "Really? But what I said to them was true, no? And, actually, *actually*, what I'm really doing is trying my best not to get involved."

"How do you expect not to be involved when you are the Head of School in which it happened?"

"Yes, no, but, I mean, you were at the meeting yesterday, right? You saw that most of the staff were sympathetic to Yunus's plight? I know you aren't, but –"

"That's not in fact true," Redman said. "But I don't see why Lorraine should suffer collateral damage for just doing her job. Yunus seems to have put himself in the position he's in."

Matthews placed an agitated hand on his forehead. "There was a lot of collateral damaged at yesterday's staff meeting, James. It ended in a blood bath once you and Donald got at it. That's one reason I think it best not to get further involved."

"But you *have* to do something about *this*, Bernard," Redman insisted. "You can't stand by while your own School administrator is getting anonymous threats and obscenities. Go and see Asterisk."

"The Registrar?" Matthews grimaced. "I tried that yesterday morning. He virtually kicked me out of his office and told me it was nothing to do with me and that I should stay clear of it."

"What he meant was that you should stay clear of the Yunus business. But he'll be sympathetic about *this*."

Matthews pondered for a moment, glancing longingly at the text of D. H. Lawrence's "The Primrose Path" on his monitor. "No, really, it's all too complicated. What would I say to him? What could he do? I don't think he has a lot of time for me."

Redman's nostrils flared. "Alright, *I* will go and see him."

Matthews brightened. "Really? Would you? Well, that would be capital! Anything that might get Lorraine back to work sooner rather than later would be very welcome. And the Registrar speaks highly of you. Must be all that, er, Union work you used to do."

Redman turned on his heel, but before he left he looked back at Matthews once more. "For what it's worth, if you get any more media calls, I suggest making no comment."

Matthews' face was already half-hidden behind his screen again, his hands poised above the keyboard. He looked up briefly, nodded agreeably and piped, "Wilco!"

Redman had no problem getting to talk to Asterisk these days, but on this occasion it was particularly easy. Within seconds of his calling the Registrar's secretary, Alison Stilt, he was put through directly. When Asterisk came on the line he was peculiarly warm.

"James," he said. "How opportune that you should call just at this moment. Something's come up on which I would value your thoughts. Can you come over right now, by any chance?"

Within sixty seconds he had crossed the quadrangle and was sitting in front of Asterisk's enormous desk, beside Drusilla Frost, the University's Director of Communications, who seemed a little miffed that he had been asked to join her meeting with Asterisk *in medias res*. They exchanged stiff hellos.

There are four things modern senior university managements look for in a Head of Public Relations: absolute loyalty (to management, that is, rather than to the staff below them or to the institution as a collective entity); unquestioning obedience; a flair for knowingly telling lies without compunction; and a decided photogenicity (because cameras are often involved). Any three of these qualities is sufficient for success in such a role, and only mendacity, strictly speaking, is un-negotiable. But woe betide the PR man or woman whose stock falls to possession of merely two of these characteristics: he or she is at that point on his or her way out.

Drusilla Frost had occupied her position for a very long time because, uniquely, for most of her incumbency under Covet, she had possessed all four. Now in her late forties, however, her looks were beginning to slide, and she had taken to disguising their deterioration with increasingly fetching forms of dress and coiffure. Today she was wearing a chastely seductive cashmere twin set and slacks, and her dark black hair was gathered at the back in an immaculate chignon designed to reveal hooped gold earrings. Upon Covet's death and through-out the several weeks of media fire-fighting which had ensued, Drusilla had become accustomed to operating without the usual checks on her from above. She now felt that she ran pretty much her own show, indeed on some days the entire show, and in this period of temporary independence her capacity for permanent obedience to her superiors had declined even more sharply than her erstwhile beauty. Asterisk had of necessity seen a lot of her in these three months, felt indebted to her for helping him hold the baby, and had become a little bewitched by the delicate and arousing scent of Chanel which surrounded her like a magnetic field, as well as the deep Anne Bancroft voice and her svelte, still gracious figure. Redman, by contrast, held her in a contempt which, over the years, had been more than reciprocated.

"James," Asterisk began, "I don't know if you are aware, but there was a press release yesterday –"

"Oh yes," said Redman. "I've read it." He held up the copy of *The Guardian*, which he had brought with him. "Lots of it is in here, word for word, this morning."

"Oh!" said Drusilla with dismay. "You've seen that."

"Yes," said Redman. "And of course, the members of staff named in it are now being called by the rest of the media. In fact, Nigel, that's what I wished to talk to you about."

"I see," said Asterisk, with a forced smile. "I should have guessed that I had no need to get you up to speed. It happened, after all, in your School."

"Yes," said Redman. "I even witnessed the first arrest with my own eyes, as did half of my School colleagues."

"Do you," Asterisk ventured, "have a view on the, er, affair so far?"

"Yes," Redman said. "I think the arrests were perfectly understandable, and I wish to save my colleagues from being crucified in public for their association with them – especially the School administrator, Lorraine Quant, who reported the matter to you in the first place, as it was her duty to do, and is now receiving hate mail as a result of her good judgment, and thanks to *The Guardian* naming her, of course. She's just had to go home because of the shock and worry it has caused her."

Asterisk tutted and shook his head in sympathy. Then he looked at Drusilla. "You see? I did say we could rely on good sense and balance in some quarters."

Drusilla nodded and turned to Redman with a practised smile that suggested she was turning down the level of refrigeration she usually maintained in his presence.

"James," she said, her vocal chords suddenly producing the deep tones of cordiality she turned on only in moments when she recognised a potential ally, "this press release, do you have any idea of its source? It bears no contact information."

Redman was slightly on his guard, not least because he felt himself once more too close to a natural enemy for comfort.

"Not really," he answered, "though the 'academic who is familiar with the arrested student' is almost certainly his supervisor, Brad Gooltree. As you might expect, the arrests were discussed at length in the staff meetings yesterday of the two Schools involved. So I'd guess that the authors originate in one or both of those Schools. It's a document designed to recruit others to a cause, obviously, and by turning its demands into a petition it's essentially sounding a clarion call for an ongoing campaign around some very controversial terms which are like chimes of doom to all non-thinking liberals: Islamophobia, academic freedom and, dare I say, though he's not been mentioned yet, Donald Trump? No responsible newspaper should have reproduced it without any indication of source, but after last term Odium is a sitting duck it's deemed fair to fire at outside the normal rules of engagement. I'd say you can expect a lot more, and a lot worse."

Drusilla moved her head up and down, seemingly appreciative of the warning. "The press release says nothing about the School administrator or the Schools involved, yet the author of this *Guardian* article obviously got that information in addition somehow."

"Well," said Redman, "the release would have been sent with a covering email which possibly offered more information and probably a contact number for comment also. It's a hand-in-glove deal. The article says nothing about the source of the information because the reporter is hoping for more fuel for the fire later."

"So," said Drusilla, "if we looked at emails sent out from both of those Schools yesterday..."

Redman waved his hand in negation and disapproval. "No. Forgive me, but I think you are going along entirely the wrong track if what you are seeking to do is stifle this story at source, not least because a freedom-of-speech flag has now been stuck in it. Imagine what prying into people's emails will do to enflame that issue. In any case, it was probably sent from a private email address, not a University one. The story is out there now, for better or worse. It's now about managing it, keeping it in proportion."

Drusilla seemed a little piqued at Redman's dismissal of her suggestion, but Asterisk stepped in to rescue her.

"As you can tell, James, this has taken us a little unawares," he said. "We did not expect quite such a sudden and public overreaction and it's the last thing we want, of course, having just recovered from, er, what happened last term. Now these demands, which are going to be petitioned for, well, they are inflammatory and unreal and hopelessly undeliverable. We took the decision that we had to call the police, and the police are usually cooperative with us, but as soon as they arrived we lost all the influence over them that we seem to have over more minor matters. Terrorism, or suspected terrorism, seems to fling them into a different set of frenzied routines, and an entirely different set of people seem to have got involved – CID, Special Branch, not PC Plod and Sergeant Smith. All the police currently on campus are not here questioning people because we want them to be. They've just swarmed here of their own accord. We couldn't stop them if we tried."

"I know," said Redman. "I saw that during the first arrest. They paid no heed to Elfyn at all, even when he was just trying to talk to them."

Drusilla seemed to have recovered from her momentary annoyance. She perked up.

"So," she said, "and correct me if I am wrong, James, you seem to be agreeing with us that it would be good if we could find a way to take the wind out of this campaign's sails?"

"Well, of course," Redman answered, "but not by trying to identify and silence its orchestrators. They would simply use such a move as evidence of the very censoriousness the campaign is opposing."

"What if there were another way?"

"Like what?"

"Well," she said, "we have a video."

"Ah," said Redman, "you mean the video of Yunus giving oral sex to Faraj?"

Drusilla was genuinely startled.

"How do you know it's Faraj?" she demanded.

"Believe me," said Redman, "it's Faraj."

"Wow!" exclaimed Drusilla. "Even better!"

Redman narrowed his eyes at her in disbelief. "You can't be serious, Drusilla. You can't be suggesting going public with that video."

"Well, not directly, not ourselves," she explained. "More of having it 'leaked' and then having to react to it when prompted."

"But Drusilla," Redman protested, "that's a private matter between two consenting adults. It's not fair game."

"Huh!" Drusilla jerked her head back dismissively. "It wasn't very private, was it? It was stored on a University hard drive and, if I'm not mistaken, the Odium logos in the background and the office furniture rather con-clusively prove that it was filmed in his own office in your School. I even went in there and checked the layout and the angles and everything. Now there's an instant sacking offence if ever I came across one."

"No, no," Redman persisted. "It's beyond all decency, Drusilla."

"Yes!" she agreed. "It *is* beyond all decency! And I imagine its revelation will create a massive withdrawal of sympathy for both of them. Don't you? Two gay Muslims, *in flagrante*? It's dynamite!"

"Please!" Redman turned to Asterisk. "Do not do this to him. It would destroy Yunus, maybe Faraj too. Think of their families, their friends."

"The thing is," Asterisk explained, "we have to sack him, and we have to sack him today. The police are absolutely categorical that the last stamp in his passport is faked. They told us this morning, and with that knowledge and no countervailing evidence, we can't continue to employ him beyond today. If we sack him because he is illegal, it looks bad for us. He's been with us almost a year and we failed to do due diligence. But if we sack him for gross misconduct –"

"But don't you see?" Redman pleaded. "The campaign will then be about homophobia as well as Islamophobia. You'll have the gay rights lobby down on you as well – as it were. How bad do you want this to get?"

"Bottom line," said Drusilla, "we want this campaign strangled at birth, or at least before Trump comes."

"That's never going to happen, Drusilla," Redman countered. "It's possible that Yunus and Faraj might not even be released before Trump comes, and the longer the police hold them, the more this campaign will build and build. Even if they are released, the campaign will then rally around them in person, making them into symbols for this soft-in-the-head 'humane' liberal consensus that the students and a lot of the staff mistake for real politics.

There'll be a lot of carnival and drama because, basically, there are teenagers involved, middle-aged ones as well as actual ones. You can't extinguish this overnight. All you can do is counter it over time."

Drusilla shook her head. "I say we go for the jugular. It's the quickest way. It's efficient and direct, even if there is a lot of blood. Bang bang, they're dead."

Redman suddenly had a brainwave. He looked to Asterisk.

"Have you run this idea past the VC yet?"

"Not yet. Of course, I intend to."

"Have you given thought to how he might react to it? I mean, of how he might feel *personally* about a proposal to out and shame two gay men in this way?"

Asterisk looked instantly uneasy.

Redman rubbed the point home. "It might not be a good idea even to suggest it to him."

Asterisk sat back and thought new thoughts. "Actually, Drusilla, I think James may have a good point."

Drusilla sighed impatiently. "Then what? What's the immediate next step?" she implored.

"I suggest," Redman continued, "that if you have to sack him, you sack him on the immigration issue and simply take that on the chin. I don't have too much sympathy for him on the job front, to be sure. He was apparently pretty useless. This way it appears to be no more than incompetence on your part, a failure to check one person's paperwork in a large organisation with thousands of staff, but it's clearly deliberate deception on his. The police will get all the opprobrium for pursuing the immigration issue like the petty bureaucrats they are, not you: you can honestly say that your hands were tied. Quite what happens to Yunus after that I don't know, and honestly I don't think we should care. He might be deported pretty swiftly and then you won't have him to deal with any longer. As to the campaign, you undermine it, but you won't be successful if all you deploy are officious managerial statements that are simply pious and don't engage with people's concerns. For a start, you can point to the hate speech that is being directed at your own members of staff and you can rally directly to their defence. These people are victimised individuals. Here are two examples, put under Lorraine Quant's door just this morning. These are the originals."

He passed the two notes to Asterisk, and went on.

"Then you get non-aligned members of staff, not the usual obvious stooges or yes-men, to make a public statement defending the University from the charges this press release and petition make. You *do not* – no offence, Drusilla – turn this into a routine, mechanical PR exercise. You have to form an opposition which can rally around your ideas and your discourse, not quite the way the other side are going to create events and spectacles for the media circus, but you have to get beyond simply issuing press statements *ex cathedra* and thinking they will have any effect. Don't expect to win. You'll take a big hit, you'll be defeated in the eyes of *Guardian*-reading liberal public opinion. But you can foil them, you can point to the excesses they will indulge in and the stupidities they will utter. But to do so, you have to engage, you have to abandon the cynical Olympian aloofness which is your default mode in these situations, you have to show that you are standing up for a set of positive values that it may be harder to have petitions and letter-writing campaigns about, that are less glamorous but actually more vital. You have to be prepared to articulate a positive idea of a university that isn't just the usual verbal slick and gloss. As far as I can tell, an approach like that should chime with the VC, no?"

Asterisk was looking more positive. "I do like the sound of this. But, you know, it's easier said than done, for us. To be blunt, James, with a few exceptions like yourself, well, and I'm sure Drusilla wouldn't even contradict me when I say it, the stooges and the yes-men are the ones we tend to deal with."

There was a silence. Redman stared at Asterisk with some accusation in the look.

"Nigel," he said, with the determined air of someone calling in a promise, "you and I had a meeting last November after Covet's death, and you told me things were going to be different. You told me you wanted to run this place with a renewed sense of decency."

Asterisk looked rather sheepish at this reminder being voiced in front of Drusilla, who did well to conceal any outward reaction. Nonetheless, he replied, "That's true. I did. And I do. It's just that, if we are to follow your advice on this issue, we could do with your knowledge of how things work on the ground here, which, there's no point pretending otherwise, is better than ours."

Redman held Asterisk's eye for a moment, until he was satisfied as to his good faith.

"Alright," he replied.

Chapter Seven

McNamara had not told Redman the entire truth about the contents of the last envelope he had received from Cannon Buckrack. He had deduced that it must be from Buckrack because it contained the invoices which proved that the three "Odiumgate" microdevices had been purchased on Asterisk's budget. Buckrack, he knew, had entered Asterisk's office to remove these invoices, though the assumption that he and Redman had made was that Buckrack had done so with a view to covering up their existence, whereas it now seemed that the American's intention had been, on the contrary, precisely to reveal it. But inside the package was also a copy of Jane Blake's Public Interest Disclosure. When Redman gave him this document a few days later, having received it from Asterisk, McNamara had deliberately feigned ignorance of it. Yet he had read and re-read it many times already, with near-total bafflement at the account it gave of her relations with him, which did not correspond to his perceptions in the slightest and seemed completely made up. And there was yet a third item in the package whose receipt he had hidden from everyone. It was a small black thumb drive which contained only one file – a video file.

When McNamara read Jane's document on that November Saturday morning, he had no idea that Jane and Covet were at that very moment beginning to decompose simultaneously in Covet's country cottage. He presumed that it had been sent, like the previous documents, as a revelation, a means by which Buckrack could blow the gaff on Covet as he had done before, by using McNamara as his conduit. The video of Covet and Jane having sex in the hotel – which McNamara had watched, of course, open-mouthed and astonished – seemed to have been enclosed as verification that her Public Interest Disclosure was indeed truthful, and McNamara imagined that Jane had somehow contrived to make the video with a view to securing such proof. It was absolutely clear from the film itself that she had positioned the camera deliberately, that she was playing to it, and that Covet was not aware of its presence.

He found himself in a mental paralysis for several hours because, while he knew how Buckrack had come into possession of all the documents, he could think of no satisfactory explanation for how he had also acquired the video, unless he had somehow stolen it from her, which would be an act consistent with the little that McNamara already knew of Buckrack's behaviour. But if Buckrack had done so, did Jane know? Yet how could Buckrack be connected to her in so personal a way that he could have done such a thing? Buckrack's intentions now seemed clear enough: while acting as if he were an agent of Covet's, he had in fact been surreptitiously aiming to expose Covet's wrongdoing all along, although why he would wish to do so was a mystery. The delivery of the video to McNamara was presumably to be explained as the passing on of ultimate evidence of the Vice Chancellor's misdeeds for McNamara to use in order to destroy him. Beyond that knowledge, however, he knew nothing at all about Buckrack, who was a mere phantom without solid substance in McNamara's mind, a faceless, insubstantial ghost who had merely pushed incriminating documents his way. But this – this video – was an obscenity, and a divulgence too far. Any person who shared it would become enravelled in its salacious repugnance, and McNamara had virtually discounted the idea of telling anyone about it the moment he saw it. He was by nature a bottler-up rather than a pourer-forth.

Jane Blake may have been no saint, indeed it appeared she was more the opposite of a saint than McNamara had ever envisioned, and yet he had known her, he had spent time with her, he had had everyday conversations with her, and he had found her inoffensive, even sweet, and certainly seeming-chaste in her behaviour towards him, at least. Although Covet had increasingly appeared like the Devil come to earth in human form – an impression which her document and the video redoubled in force – he felt intuitively that using the film to expose Covet would be to wrong her most cruelly, unless it were perversely her wish.

In the evening, after much thought, he decided to try to find out. He called her mobile number.

To his confusion, the call was answered up by a gravelly male English voice.

"Hello," McNamara said. "Could I talk to Jane?"

"May I ask to whom I am speaking?" replied the man, over-formal.

"It's Professor McNamara. Could you pass her to me, please?"

"That would be Jane Blake you're after, sir?"

"That's right," said McNamara, becoming slightly puzzled at the officiousness of the responses at the other end.

"Could you hold just a moment, sir?"

There was the muffled sound of a hand being placed over the mouthpiece and then a different man's voice came on the line.

"Hello, sir, this is Detective Superintendent Nesbit of the Buckinghamshire CID. Can I ask how you know Ms Blake?"

"CID?" McNamara was taken aback. "Is she in some kind of trouble? Why do you have her phone?"

"Well, sir, the most I can say at the moment is that she is part of an enquiry. You know the young woman, sir? You say your name is, er, McNamara?"

"Professor Robert McNamara." He was then asked to spell his name. "Yes, she's a postgraduate student at the University of Odium, where I work. She lives in a student residence I am responsible for. She's a Hall Tutor, which means she helps look after the undergraduates."

"Well, yes, that certainly tallies with the documentation we have. So you are her employer?"

"Not exactly," McNamara replied. "But sort of."

"And you were calling her why?"

McNamara improvised. "I just needed to speak to her about some business in the Hall," he said.

"I see, sir. Well, I am glad you called, because we have been trying to get hold of someone at the University who might help us but, it being a Saturday, we are not having much luck. We were really hoping to speak with a person who knows her."

"Well, I do know her, naturally."

"Then, sir, if it wouldn't be asking too much, is it at all possible that you could come down here now, I mean to Buckinghamshire? I cannot stress how urgent it is. It's a couple of hours' drive, but I can have a car sent to pick you up immediately. And they shall of course return you afterwards."

McNamara went. An hour later he was sweeping past Northampton and then Milton Keynes in a police car with two Odium police constables who knew nothing of the purpose of their drive and could not enlighten him. He was not even certain which Buckinghamshire town they arrived at, and failed to ask, so bewildered was he by the turn of events. He was delivered to the underground car park of a large grey police station, where the Detective Superintendent was waiting to meet him.

Nesbit was a polite man, circumspect, but routine, obviously experienced in dealings of this kind.

"To be honest with you, Professor McNamara, it's really no more than positive identification we require at the moment. We have two bodies here in our morgue, a middle-aged man and a young woman. We are pretty sure who the man is on account of the property at which the bodies were found, though if you can help us with either or both I would be grateful."

"You want me to identify dead bodies?" McNamara repeated, stunned into disbelief.

"Yes, sir, if you wouldn't mind? We need to try and resolve this matter quickly so that we can inform relatives. Could you come with me? The morgue is on this level, and I'll try not to keep you long. I do warn you, it may not be pleasant."

He was led to the cold mortuary, where an attendant unceremoniously slid Jane Blake's dead body out of a deep-freeze compartment. McNamara gazed upon her ashen-white face, which seemed like a poor half-finished waxwork facsimile of her, eyes closed, dark discoloured blood staining her neck and clotted in her long brown hair, as well as in what he could see of her clothes around the shoulders. The sight rendered him speechless for several moments. His bowels rumbled.

"Is this Jane Blake, sir?" Nesbit asked after a respectful pause.

"Yes," McNamara blurted out weakly.

Nesbit made to have the body put away again almost immediately.

"The man, sir, as I say, we are fairly confident of his identity, but I wonder...?"

McNamara was beset by waves of adrenalin and shock. His legs felt weak. He managed to stutter, "Yes, yes, of course."

Covet's body, though bloodless, was even more disquietingly ghastly. The features were twisted in a caricature of pain, all asymmetrical, and there was a violent brown welt around his neck.

"Evan Covet?" Nesbit asked expectantly.

"Sir Evan Covet," McNamara replied. "He's the Vice Chancellor of the University."

"Oh, *Sir* Evan Covet?" Nesbit repeated. "I see. That's useful. Did you know him well?"

McNamara shook his head.

"And the young woman?" Nesbit went on. "When did you last see her?"

McNamara tried to cast his mind back. "Come to think of it, not for a while. Maybe two weeks? I can't be absolutely sure."

"That's alright," said Nesbit gently. "It's usually a bit of a shock, this kind of thing. We can always speak later. Tell me, did she ever give you any indication that she was in a relationship with this man, with, er, *Sir* Evan?"

McNamara shook his head, aware that his denial was technically true but that it concealed a great deal of knowledge that he had recently acquired.

"Was she?" he asked disingenuously.

Nesbit seemed indecisive about how much he should divulge, but finally confirmed, "It looks that way from evidence at the scene. It's a bit early in the proceedings and we're still piecing things together, but it appears, most likely, to be a crime of passion."

McNamara gestured with both hands in the direction of both bodies. "What happened?"

Nesbit's mouth twisted to the side as if he had already said too much. "There's not a lot I can say at this stage. It's an ongoing investigation."

"But," said McNamara, "all the blood?"

"Oh, the lady?" Nesbit tapped his solar plexus. "Single knife wound. And the, er, gentleman, well, as you probably could see, it looks like asphyxiation by hanging. Not an unusual combination when there are two bodies involved."

"Not unusual?" McNamara echoed incredulously. "Not unusual, you say?"

Nesbit smiled, but kept the smile small, decently contained. "Not unusual in my line of business, I meant, sir. Obviously a bit of a jolt for a civilian like yourself. Where there's a double death like this, it's often murder followed by a suicide."

"You're saying," murmured McNamara, his shock deepening still further, "that he *stabbed* her, then *hanged* himself?" He felt close to stupefaction now, hardly able to think straight at all. His upset evidently showed, because Nesbit put a steadying hand on his elbow.

"No, Professor McNamara, not for sure, it's more me just thinking aloud. There are further forensics for us to do, and there will have to be post-mortems. We'll know more then. But it's hardly the first time I have seen something like this."

"I don't understand," McNamara said. "Why here? Buckinghamshire?"

"The deceased gentleman owned a property nearby," said Nesbit. "That's where we found them."

It did not take much longer. McNamara was surprised how few questions the Detective Superintendent wanted to ask, but in fact Nesbit seemed more concerned to let him go, and expressed his gratitude sincerely more than once.

"Oh," said McNamara on the way out, remembering something through his turbulence of feeling and perplexity of mind. "It just occurred to me to say, I also saw him personally, Sir Evan, and more recently, a week or so ago. No, a little more than a week. It was very unusual. He called me early in the morning and asked me to drive out to his home near Odium. He wanted to speak with me about *her*, about Jane. He told me she had lodged some kind of formal complaint with the University. He wasn't clear, but he seemed to want my advice."

"A written complaint, sir? Do you know what it was about?"

"He said it was about sexual harassment, but he was rather vague on the details. These things are usually treated very confidentially. He wanted to know about her state of mind. I told him she seemed normal to me, although I found it very strange that he was involving himself in the matter. Then later that day, or perhaps it as the day after, it was made public that he had been suspended from work. You should contact the University Registrar. He will know more. His name is Dr Nigel Asterisk."

"That's very useful to know," said Nesbit, writing the name down.

"He can also help you with her contact details. She's American, by the way."

"Yes," Nesbit replied, "we have her passport."

"Can you," McNamara asked tentatively, "keep my name out of it? Dr Asterisk and I do not, how can I put it, get on. I'd rather not have to account to him. This is going to cause chaos, and I'd prefer not be dragged into it."

Nesbit considered this request for a moment and replied evenly, "Of course, sir. I see no reason why not. You've been extremely helpful to us."

The detective then accompanied him to the waiting police car. He asked McNamara to say nothing to anyone about the matter until a firmer conclusion had been reached, and expressed his thanks yet once more. Then, as a parting word, and with some genuine pathos, he added, "She was only twenty-three. She seemed a fine-looking girl. In life, I mean. Not so much in death."

Those were the last words Nesbit exchanged with him. The policeman never, in fact, called on him again.

On the journey back to Odium, McNamara found himself sliding into a deep depression for which he could not find a word. It was not grief, nor was it loss, but a profound sorrow at life wasted, of vitality despoiled, of a promising future annihilated. He was touched to the quick by the snuffing out of Jane's being, and by the time he reached home his resolve to say nothing to anyone about the video or her Disclosure had become an inflexible determination. He weirdly felt that he owed it to her that her name and her memory be no more damaged than they already were. She had already suffered the most extreme penalty possible for the follies she had committed. What point would there be in besmirching her further?

He locked and chained his doors, drank half a bottle of

scotch, and went to bed.

It was that night that his bad dreams began.

He found himself in the Senior Common Room of Coolwipe Hall with Jane Blake sitting across from him, as she had been on the last evening he had seen her alive. He was appraising her sexually, she knew it, she was encouraging it, and he was liking it. She stood up, crossed the room to him with a few elegant steps, and got down on her knees before his half-reposing form.

Imperiously, in exactly the mode in which Covet had preferred to speak to her in the video, he began to order her to please him according to his whim.

"Bare your breasts," he said confidently.

Slowly, smiling like a votary, she undid the buttons of her shirt one-by-one, then parted the silky fabric to allow him to admire her dark, stiff nipples.

"Jiggle my junk," he ordered.

She compliantly unzipped him and eased his balls and cock out into view. She took his member in her right hand and gently stroked it, watching it grow with an admiration bordering on devotion.

"Tongue my titan," he commanded manfully.

She giggled and kissed his scrotum, allowing his enlarged bratwurst to rest on her face, where it balanced on her nose and was sandwiched between her eyes. Then she put out her tongue and allowed it to travel the length of his now-stiffened meat stick, a manoeuvre she repeated several times for his delectation.

"Suck that sausage," he encouraged arrogantly.

As if he were granting her a great privilege, she bent forward a little and wrapped her lips around his swollen thundersword, stroking it moistly as she slid her lips back and forth along it. McNamara closed his eyes and put his hands behind his head in supreme delight, allowing the pleasure to course through his veins.

"That's it," he whispered. "Blow me!"

All at once she stopped, and withdrew his majesty from her mouth. He opened his eyes to look at her with the scornful disapproval of a short-changed customer. She was still hovering close to his exposed elephant. However, she appeared no longer as the perfectly primed sex bomb of the video. Without warning, the face on her slackening body had become that of the grotesque, cinereous, ugly heap on the mortuary slab, except that its eyes moved and its other features twitched, zombie-like.

Horror began to well up within him. Her expression was becoming more sour and minatory by the second.

With an inspiration whose origin he could not fathom, McNamara found himself now commanding, "Blow that babymaker!"

Jane's face quickly re-assumed, film-special-effects-like, its living lineaments. Vital colours rapidly resurged into her flesh. She began to smile flirtatiously once more, and leaned forward again to take his chopper in her chops.

"Fellate my phallus," he essayed.

She fellated.

"Flange that fleshtower!" he exclaimed, with renewed self-possession.

She flanged.

"Feast on my fuckmutton!" he cried triumphantly.

She feasted.

Intransitive verbs were apparently accepted coinage in this exchange, he concluded. Would it work, he wondered, if he cheated on the alliteration?

"Shmoke my shaft," he gambled experimentally.

She halted forthwith. He was looking at the brown crown of her stilled head and could already see the hair fading and becoming desiccated. He could feel in her lip-grip a new unwillingness which suggested that a second erection-chilling interruption was about to occur.

"Quaff from my quiverbone!" he ordered anew.

She readily resumed, with clear intent to quaff.

"Siphon that soldier!"

He started to sense the slow, satisfying semblance of incipient siphoning.

"Drain that drillhammer!" he bellowed in ecstasy.

As he ejaculated he heard the brassy booming of Wagner's "Ride of the Valkyries" surging from the distance, but this turned out to be no more than a deformation of his mobile ringtone, which eventually bounced him into consciousness.

It was Redman, telling him about the death of Covet being reported in the Sunday papers. McNamara held a brief discussion with him on the phone, during which he felt the warm wetness between his stomach and the sheets turn cold. Redman came round an hour later and the crapulent McNamara, with his head pounding, held another fitful, disjointed conversation with him. Mc-Namara dissembled lack of interest. He likewise said nothing about his visit to Buckinghamshire the previous evening, partly in observance of Nesbit's injunction, but also because it was strongly associated in his hungover brain with the disturbance he felt at the dream he had just had. He gave Redman the invoices and they agreed how Redman would deal with Asterisk in respect of them. Redman left, and they did not see one another until several nights later.

During those several nights, McNamara kept the dead Jane alive in his dreams with the embalming fluid she extracted from his sappy cucumber in obedience to his very deliberately worded imperatives. In wildly mixed-metaphorical wet dreams, his nocturnal self plumbed the nether regions of the alliterative lexicon of love, while the drip-fed Jane Blake duly plumbed his nether regions. She tickled his tallywhacker, massaged his microphone, and frotted his firehose. When she had finished kindling his candle by rubbing his roger, she devoured his dragon, hoovered his heatseeker, and would even (phonetics regularly trumping orthography) keenly nosh on his knob yet capriciously decline to guzzle on his gigi. She fed at his fudgehole and, bungholing his banger, proceeded to poopchute his piston. Thereafter, she needed little persuasion to cockholster his cumgun or leather his longfellow, with the consequence that his joystick was inevitably jizzcreeked. The pampered Professor awoke each morning with a bishop like a badly bent boomerang.

He called in sick and spent the days alone. Rachel Brace, Asterisk's ex-secretary, the living woman of his own age with whom he had been falling in love a mere week or two before, called several times, but he put her off. He would go through these days feeling fits of crestfallen self-reproach at the Covetousness which had arisen within him, which mounted at times to the delusion that somehow Sir Evan's damaged soul had at death transmigrated into him, forcing his own out like an invading cuckoo. But as darkness approached he became more like a vampire in a coffin, looking forward leeringly to the orgy of the senses with Jane which each new witching hour promised.

Then one night, the night he next saw Redman, he could not get to sleep. Redman brought news from the outside, from a world that seemed to McNamara to have retreated to the horizon, news such as Redman having convinced Asterisk that Jane Blake's Disclosure could not be made public as it would most likely give rise to lawsuits from Sergei Krokoff and Avril Poon, and that such further scandals would destroy the modest opportunity there now was for Odium to rebuild after the shattering earthquake it had suffered. When Redman passed him a copy of the Disclosure he already possessed, conscience awoke, and McNamara finally told him, swearing him to secrecy, about his trip to the morgue the previous weekend, and blamed that for his obviously poor state of mind and morale. Redman was touchingly sympathetic and promised to help keep the world yet longer at bay. He would, for example, have a discreet word with Rachel. He would tell Asterisk to call Frank Dashwood and let him know that McNamara would not be reporting for work for a few weeks. Asterisk seemed eager to comply, these days, with any recommendation Redman had to make.

When Redman departed, McNamara felt for a while that what he had said to the younger man might be true, and that all he might need in order to recover was the time and the relief that Redman would secure. He had suffered a trauma. Surely the dreamer was not morally responsible for the content of his dreams, however ignoble they were? Yet he was sensitive to his own deceit. He knew that his waking self had been altered too, indeed even now he was savouring the hypnotic feeling of libidinal corruption at the thought that, in only an hour or two, he might once more get to enjoy all kinds of cock-roguery with the succubus Jane.

Yet Jane would not come because sleep would not come, which meant that McNamara could not come. He tossed and turned for close to two hours, before a solution presented itself which was suitably un-scrupulous. He pulled open a bedside drawer in which he had thrown a small baggie of marijuana he had confiscated from a student in Coolwipe Hall earlier that evening. He would normally have called Security and passed it to them, but his current hermit-like instincts had governed his choice, and he had decided to procrastinate. There was a generous amount of ganja in the baggie. A preliminary tryst with Mary Jane, he reflected wryly, might ease him in his passage to the faerie Jane.

He had to dress and make a trip to a local garage for tobacco and rolling papers. Back in his bedroom, he constructed a classic elongated doobie which, although double-wrapped, seemed to him makeshift and crooked, exhibiting none of the conical perfection routinely achieved in the past by his younger, nimbler fingers. Nonetheless, it burned well, and after a few hot inhalations he felt the old, light, paradisal excitement start gently to suffuse his limbs and permeate his brain. A few drags later, his found himself gently stroking the head of his little brother and smiling, not simply to himself, but beaming idiotically at the empty darkened room. By the end of the joint he had coaxed the Little Boy into being a Fat Man, standing up straight with the aid of the iPad, the dead Jane and the dead Covet, and disregard of the moral questions raised by virtual necrophilia. For much of the video Covet's face was not in shot, so it was not altogether impossible for McNamara to imagine himself in the then-enviable position of the then-VC, especially if he turned down the audio.

McNamara took his time. Two or three gigglesticks later, something occurred which he did not recall from his youth. As a teenager he had found the experience of spliffing largely valuable from a cerebral point of view, delightfully disarranging his thoughts and modes of thinking. But now it seemed more physical, in that it made him all arousal and goose-flesh and nipple-stiffened and irresistibly libidinal, to which a larger-than-usual, and indescribably intenser-than-usual jizzplosion eventually testified. It was an emission on a mission. And its objective was to splash itself onto the two-dimensional naked form of Jane Blake, conveniently miniaturised on the screen he held before his standing-to-attention lap-soldier. It was accompanied by his genuinely involuntary cry of surprised bliss brought on by its unmistakably elongated rapture. Drained of all energy in a moment, McNamara was barely able to discard the iPad on the bedside desk before collapsing back onto his pillows in a fuggy warm glow, which carried him, gently but euphorically, towards a deep and uninterrupted night-long sleep.

Superior orgasms followed by truly restorative and unbroken rest? What man in his sixtieth year would not embrace the medicinal plant which offered both, especially one following immediately upon the other? Within a week McNamara had doubled his on-hand supply of weed, courtesy of some rigorous sniffing-out of offenders in the Hall. At some point in the next month, a little despondent at the predictable downturn in sensation caused by his regular nightly toking and stroking, he discovered and purchased from Amazon a revolutionary masturbation gadget, made in Japan and called the Tenga Fliphole, a marvel of engineering which reproduced in latex the design of the human vagina (encased in a sturdy plastic-hand-holdable and warm-water-washable housing) and provided a leak-proof container for his testicular outpourings, as well as making McNamara newly grateful that he lived in the twenty-first century.

He soon grew tired of the repetitiveness of Jane's

video as sole stimulus. But it did not take him long to find a porn actress, among the cast of thousands freely on offer, who approximated to Jane's looks and body morphology, if anything even improved upon them, and who flaunted herself in better light, was captured with much more varied camera work, and whose cinematic *oeuvre* was so plentiful it seemed, for his practical purposes, unending.

Nights passed in the company of the Jane surrogate, the lubricated Fliphole, his lop-sided joints and his straightened and pampered member, just as each day passed in anticipation of their all getting together again to party very soon. He had not reckoned, however, with the Christmas recess. By the middle of December the student body melted away, the Hall emptied, and there was an instantaneous famine of dope. McNamara soon ran out and spent a disconsolate, depressed, sleep-deprived night whose flattening, enervating effects he had almost forgotten. Chastened and craving, he idled for an entire morning, wondering how he was to cope for the whole of Christmas and New Year like this, when a fix for both his compromised sexual and psychotropic habits prompted itself salvationally from the depths of his inner travel agent.

Amsterdam was colder than Odium, but McNamara made things more comfortable for himself by not mucking about with budget options. He took a deluxe room for two weeks in the Grand Hotel Krasnapolsky, right on Dam Square. Cannabis cafés and weed-retailing establishments are a few hundred metres away, some of them with microscopes through which you can eye before you buy. Much the same is true of the red light district, which is even closer: the girls stand in lingerie behind glass doors, in full view of the human traffic perambulating past on the canal sides. McNamara was excited to discover that there was an entire terrace of Hispanic harlotry, and when he had located a girl who approximated once more to the phenomenology of Jane Blake, he responded to her moues and shaken cleavage by opening the door and engaging her in conversation.

She said she was from Puerto Rico and that her name was Conchita Dentada. She was undeniably toothsome. She did not at first wish to leave her cramped cubicle, which he presumed was where she exercised most control over unpredictable customers. But it was a mere matter of money to persuade her. Once she saw his resplendent room and the thickness of his wallet, she had no trouble staying the night in his hotel bedroom. Likewise, she had no qualms about meeting any request for any manoeuvre, no matter the indignity of the position it put her in, of the language used to make it, or the fact that McNamara was often reposing with an enormous smouldering fatty between his lips while she complied likewise. He let his imagination run wild, and surprised himself by some of the obscenities he devised, though he noticed that the majority of them were linguistic rather than physical. By week two, McNamara was reflecting that he had never devoted himself so much to Eros in any one place and time; while Conchita was agog because she had never bagged so many Euros in any one place and time. She virtually moved to the Krasnapolsky and entered a state of temporary concubinage with him. McNamara determinedly treated her much worse than he had seen Covet treat Jane. Partly he was curious just to see how much sexual abjection money could buy. He even insisted that she respond to the dead girl's name, which she did. When the fortnight was over, neither of them, in truth, regretted it: McNamara on account of the experience of feeling like

Caesar, Conchita on account of the experience of not feeling poor and, in the topsy-turvy system of values they had implicitly contracted should pertain, rather impressed with herself that she had managed to attract a repeat customer for two weeks, and moreover one who had remained "faithful" to her. They even laughingly agreed to do it all again sometime, and he took her phone number and email address.

McNamara returned a few days into the new year without a shred of moral reserve, but rather a feeling of triumph: he had seen, he had conquered, and he had repeatedly come. If anything he felt complacently satiated, and for a week he moved around the house, preparing for the resumption of his duties, with a feeling close to contentment which his penis and testicles did not complainingly interrupt. By the time they did rouse themselves again, the students had returned, and the Mary Jane and the faerie Jane were once more on tap. He continued his dalliance with both until, almost exactly one month later, he took a call one evening which informed him that his father had been dead for nearly a week.

He smoked even more than usual that night, and his iPad required a soapy damp cloth the next morning, all the same.

Chapter Eight

When Redman arrived at the Vice Chancellor's office on the Friday morning, he was surprised to see that McNamara had got there before him, unusually early. McNamara was grateful at the advent of the younger man, for he had already wasted three minutes of life enjoined in idle small talk with the Vice Chancellor. Spooner's casual conversation, like that of all Vice Chancellors, was predictably dominated by the first person singular pronoun, and unremittingly sprinkled with the names of celebrities or otherwise famous people he had met. To divert himself from the droning of this drone, McNamara had taken to tilting his head so that the penises-and-scrota assemblages of the nude alabaster statuettes behind Spooner appeared to pop out of the Vice Chancellor's ears. He was excessively rewarded for this manoeuvring when Redman came through the door and Spooner turned to greet him and was thus to be seen in profile, one small parcel of genitalia seeming to sprout from the crown of his head, the other appearing to issue from his mouth.

Pleasantries were exchanged. A flurry of further chit-chat was summoned forth from Spooner to herald

Redman's arrival, from which McNamara and Redman learned that Spooner had been a friend of "Theresa's" at Oxford in the mid-seventies, that he considered his friendship with the Prime Minister merely dormant rather than extinct, and that he intended (this was said in a way that might easily have been accompanied by a wink, but was not) to make it volcanically active in the near future. McNamara neglected to look impressed; Redman tried his best to look so; both surmised from Spooner's smirking reaction that he had convinced himself that he had in fact made them so.

Spooner deftly turned the talk to business. Would Redman accept the Vice Deanship? He would. Splendid. And if the offer to be Dean of his Faculty were offered again to McNamara, would he reconsider it? As usual, McNamara seemed to rain on everyone's parade. His answer was incontestably flat: he would not. Disappointment was registered and acknowledged, although this was what everyone had been expecting, so the gestures were not unduly laboured.

What no one (except him) expected was for McNamara to add, "But..."

Spooner and Redman turned their looks towards him simultaneously.

"But," McNamara repeated, "were the offer of Pro-Vice Chancellor to be renewed, I would accept that."

Redman's eyes widened. Spooner let out a delighted guffaw.

"I have given it a great deal of consideration in light of our circumstances," McNamara went on. "I now regret my impulsive refusal of the offer. I can see that we are in extremely unusual times and that I may be useful in the office."

"That," exclaimed Spooner, nodding and smiling, "is

wonderful news! What a successful meeting!"

"There is just one condition," said McNamara, "which I hope will not seem unreasonable and which may also make a great deal of sense."

After the briefest pause, Spooner said, "I'm all ears."

"Well," said McNamara, "as we know, each PVC is given responsibility for staffing matters in a faculty other than his or her own. I'd like to have that responsibility for James's faculty, Arts. The reason should not be disguised: it means that the Dean of Arts will be in a pincer, with me directly above him and James directly below. Why do we need or want that? Because I assure you that the Dean of Arts is a fatuous oaf and that most of the trouble we are going to experience over the association with President Trump will come from staff and students in the faculties of Arts and Social Sciences. I cannot have staffing responsibility in Social Sciences, as it is my own faculty. But don't waste me on any other. It has to be Arts."

Spooner mulled this over. "It would involve a bit of a reshuffle," he thought out loud. "But look, would you be prepared to be the International PVC, in your more general role? That's what I really need right now. There's stuff to do on China, and different from what you might imagine."

McNamara spread his hands genially. "I'm happy with any general role as long as the staffing responsibility is for the Arts."

"Done!" boomed Spooner, and looked at his desk as if mourning the lack of a gavel.

"Well," said Redman afterwards in the coffee bar, "here was I thinking that the socialist shocks of history could not be surpassed after Jeremy Corbyn became leader of the Labour Party, but now we have an openly

Marxist Pro-Vice Chancellor (International) of the University of Odium, and he's already acting the part, saying, for example, not a single damn word about it before that meeting. What's going on, Robert?"

"The Arts thing was partly to support you," McNamara said laconically.

"I get that," replied Redman, "and thanks. But I still don't understand how you managed to flip over like this. You have always said you would never take a managerial role above Head of School. You've always been adamant that those above that tier lose touch with what academia is."

"I just decided that you were right. Why let someone else do it? If we want the show to be more our kind of show, we'd better start helping to direct the show, no? I'm in my sixtieth year. It hardly matters if I lose touch with academia now. I'm not planning to be in it much longer anyway. Last chance to do something different, perhaps. I assumed you'd be happy as you seem to have arrived at the same conclusion in respect of yourself."

"Well, yes, I am happy," Redman confirmed. "I just always imagined us forming a permanent opposition. I never saw us being part of *the government*."

"Speaking of which, in the ten minutes he spoke to me after asking you to leave, he told me he's got to go down to Whitehall late tomorrow afternoon for a meeting with the Minister for Higher Education and that he needs me on the China campus by Monday morning and for the rest of next week. I have to fly out tomorrow night. He made no bones about the fact that the meeting with the Minister is *about* China."

Redman took a breath. "What's afoot?"

"I'm not sure. I'm not even sure that he's sure. He said he won't be able to brief me until Sunday. The Chinese must definitely have been raising hell since last term. I mean, they were publicly denounced by a Professor of this institution. I'm assuming I am some kind of peace envoy."

"He said it would be different from what you might imagine."

McNamara grunted.

"You'll miss tomorrow's demonstration, then?" Redman added.

"What's that?" said McNamara.

Redman pulled out that morning's *Guardian* and pointed to a headline:

Student researching ISIS tactics held for four days
- Lecturers fear threat to academic freedom
- Manual downloaded from US government website

He made to hand it to McNamara but the other waved it away. "Summarise it for me," he said in disgust.

Redman warmed to the task once he had begun. "The article reveals that the student – Faraj – had sent an electronic copy of an ISIS training manual from a US government website for his research into terrorist tactics to the administrator – Yunus – so that the latter, a personal friend who had access to a printer, could print it out for him for free. Another member of staff – Lorraine – discovered the document on the administrator's computer and reported it upwards, which ultimately led to the police being called in. There's a quote from Dr Griselda Rotfang, of your School, who is Faraj's personal tutor: 'He's a serious student, who works very hard and is looking to have a career as an academic. This is of great concern for academic freedom but also for the climate on campus.' It further reports that students have begun a petition calling on the University to acknowledge 'the disproportionate nature of its response to the possession of legitimate research materials'. The reporting seems based largely on the anonymous press release I showed you the other day. The petition refers to 'radical material', of which the individuals were in possession 'for research purposes' – even though Yunus has no research remit of any kind – and calls for the University to show that it 'guarantees academic and political freedom on campus' and expresses the view that this incident constitutes 'a serious violation of academic freedom'. It ends by saying that there will be a march on campus tomorrow at 3pm in defence of academic freedom. 'Thousands are expected to attend.'"

He put the paper down. McNamara was silent. He blinked a few times, then said, "You ever been to China?"

Redman shook his head.

"It's an awful place," groaned McNamara.

"So, Drusilla," Redman found himself expounding in his office an hour later, "the defence of academic freedom is to be the rallying cry for the campaign. After all, who would *not* want to defend such a thing? It's not going to be about whether or not Yunus is legal or illegal. They are going to portray the University as a super-obedient drongo to the present illiberal state."

"But all we did," said Drusilla, "was call the police, as we are meant to do, and at that point the matter did not involve academics or students. It was only about an administrator."

"Which precisely shows your slavish, knee-jerk obedience to your political masters. The campaigners are not interested in the truth. They're interested in making politics out of nothing."

Drusilla acknowledged the circumstances with a nod. "So what should we say in this afternoon's press release?"

"Keep insisting on the truth. The reason this is a purely legal matter and not a political one is that academic freedom is exclusively the attribute and privilege of *academic staff*. It does not extend to students, not even postgraduate students, and it certainly does not extend to University administrators. The relevant University statute stipulates very clearly the categories of University members who do have academic freedom. It also specifies that the freedom it grants is for research conducted within the law."

"I'm not sure that's going to sound very *liberal*, is it?" Drusilla rejoined pointedly. "The bad spin on that is that students are second-rate citizens as far as academic freedom goes. It's never a good line, to tell people they don't have a freedom or are unequal. It makes them feel disempowered."

"It's the *truth*," said Redman exasperatedly. "That's what laws do! They define things like freedom to act and who has power to do what. But you may be right. We're probably on a hiding to nothing, especially as none of them or their student audience will pay attention to any of the media you send the press release to. The whole thing is being driven by Facebook, not by the truth."

"Nonetheless," she said, rising, "I shall have this written up and pass it by the Registrar and VC and get it out. We have to say something about this demonstration. As for what happens after the march, my office may be in touch with you for advice. Unfortunately I must be away all next week."

"Where to?" he asked.

"China," she said miserably. "There's going to be a lot of press, apparently, and they need me there. With Professor McNamara, I've just been given to understand."

Redman was gallantly helping her with her coat and made no comment.

She turned. "Forgive me," she groaned. "I know he's your colleague, but he's an awful man."

Redman and Lorraine slept late the next morning. She refused to accompany him to the campus demonstration, but Redman needed to see it with his own eyes. Despite its commencement at the late hour of three o'clock, the estimates of thousands of attendees turned out to be woefully optimistic. He calculated that there were about six hundred people at the assembly point opposite the University library. He kept aloof from both the gathering crowd and the security guards and local constables acting as marshals, watching the event from a distance. When the short serpent-like assembly set off on its winding, circuitous route around the main campus roads, he did not follow it but walked directly the four hundred yards to a small hill overlooking the march's finishing point at the Trump Building, where the University (acting under Redman's advice) had permitted a makeshift platform to be erected in the car park.

He awaited an absurdly ironic afternoon of loud unhindered public speeches condemning a lack of freedom. He did not expect, when the crowd came surging up University Drive, that each participant would have donned a tan-coloured adhesive gag, and that the mob would thus arrive in complete, melodramatic, orchestrated silence. He had been wrong. It was not simply academic freedom that would be the motivating theme but, ridiculously, grotesquely, freedom of very speech itself. The previously ideologically sleepy campus of Odium, an erstwhile playground for the offspring of the international bourgeoisie, had now, in the space of a mere term and a half, seemingly catapulted itself to the status of the British equivalent of UC Berkeley or Kent State, albeit on the basis of largely manufactured fictions rather than facts. There were press and television waiting everywhere, to the left and the right and the front of the six hundred, as they rode like a wave the final half a league of their noble charge for imagined justice.

While he was made to feel nothing like the professional in an Ian McEwan novel who smugly (and with obvious authorial approval) goes about his privileged daily life while a million people march in London to protest against their government's prosecution of an illegal war, Redman toyed with the comparison. He did so not just because it was a Saturday, but because he had an inkling that, had they been distractable from the poses they were striking, or from the incredible collective silent obedience to which they were paradoxically intent on submitting themselves, many of the students before him, some of whom he had taught and who knew him personally, would have described him as exactly such a compromised figure. Had he and his politically minded colleagues not complained for years about the lack of student activism at Odium? And yet, when it now showed itself, it did so repellently, in the most delusional of guises, a demagogic concoction no serious, reflective political person could swallow.

Two young men had been incautious in how they handled a computer file; one of them had virtually invited arrest by his provocative behaviour in front of the police; the other had consequently been discovered to be an illegal immigrant. But rather than cope with this procedurally low-level affair in which both knew that they were at fault, the two had, in order to divert attention away from their own obvious indiscretions, cooperated in magnifying it to the proportions of a racial and political scandal and persuading thousands of others – about six hundred of whom now stood as gullible sentinels to the pair's abused human rights – that the dual roots of the problem were the reactionary British state and their own entirely blameless University. In fact, it was obvious to anyone with Redman's knowledge that the real stirrer was Faraj, who, as well as being unwilling to pay for his own printing, had strutted like a trouble-seeking turkey-cock before Redman's and the police officers' eyes, and as a result had got Yunus even deeper in the legal soup than himself. And now hundreds stood to defend them, or at least to go through the vocal and physical gestures associated with such an aim, as if both were martyrs for freedom rather than a brace of posturing, chaos-causing fools.

Redman did his best to inhibit his gag reflex as Donald Doyle mounted the platform and began on a salivary Shettlestonian rant. There were plentiful cheers (the mouths seemed quickly to have abandoned their obstructing Scotch Tapes because of the perceived demand for frequent spontaneous acclaim and applause) yet Redman doubted if more than half of what he said had been understood. He was succeeded by the local constituency Labour MP, a virulent anti-Corbynite whose extra-marital affair with her Parliamentary research assistant had a month before been revealed by the *Daily Express*, and who probably was there in order to get some better press coverage for herself. She received an uproarious welcome of which Rosa Luxemburg might have been envious. She prattled and got through five minutes with slogans and clichés.

But the best was yet to come, and caused pulses of euphoria in the crowd, which more and more seemed to have assumed the characteristics and demeanour of fans at a gig just before the main megastar act. Thanks to the wonders of modern technology, Donald Doyle explained, it was possible for Yunus to speak beyond the confines of the immigration detention facility to which he had been moved that morning and in which he was now a "political prisoner". And so saying, Doyle put the microphone to the speaker of his mobile phone, whence issued the reedy voice of Yunus: "Friends, students, members of staff, fellow members of the academic community..."

Redman could not bear the burlesque for much longer. Waves of incredulous, bitter gall swept over him, almost making him dizzy. He wondered whose enforced silence it was that the gagging had been meant to symbolise. All had certainly been free with their words today and, now, even Yunus found no impediment to addressing the crowd, nor had anyone been stopped from saying pretty much anything they liked for nearly a week. Within a few minutes he had turned on his heel and was heading away from this scene of parody politics. Yunus's populist drivel, punctuated frequently by mindless applause, slowly faded from his hearing: "The Home Office conducts itself like the Gestapo. They have no respect for dignity. They treat foreigners as things. The recklessness they show is becoming of a totalitarian state. I thank all for their support. It's been heartening. I'm grateful to everyone who has helped me and shown solidarity, from students to Members of Parliament. I think this is more like the Britain we know, and not the brutal tactics of the Home Office..."

*

When McNamara opened the door of the black chauffeur-driven Lexus which called at his house late that afternoon, its back seat contained an unpleasant surprise.

"Drusilla!" he exclaimed. "What a pleasant surprise."

He got in awkwardly.

"Have you been sent to brief me on the way to the airport?" he asked.

"I've been sent to accompany you to China, Pro-Vice Chancellor. Have they not put you on the senior management email list yet?"

"Oh, for goodness sake!" he erupted tetchily.

Drusilla bridled. "I know we have had our disagreements in the past, but I didn't expect you to be so instantly oppositional to me now."

"No, you misunderstand," said McNamara. "It's the title. 'Pro-Vice Chancellor'. You cannot call me that, I will not answer to it. Neither that nor 'Professor McNamara'. We spent many years on hostile first name terms, Drusilla, so let's keep it that way."

"But without the hostility?"

"Well, of course. We're not on opposite sides of the argument now, are we? In any case, I have always assumed that you were not necessarily personally committed to the positions you had to defend when I was President of the Union branch. I was doing my job and you were doing yours."

"Gosh," she broke out. "That's the nicest thing you've ever said to me." She picked up some papers she had on her lap. "Okay. Since you are not yet on the mailing list, let me fill you in on the other big news. Have you seen the VC's letter to *The Guardian*? We eventually decided to respond to today's demonstration in that form rather than a press release."

McNamara took the paper. "This is what James Redman has been helping you with?"

Drusilla nodded. McNamara scanned the letter, reading aloud a few choice phrases. "'The incident was triggered by the discovery of an ISIS training manual on the computer of an individual who was neither an academic member of staff nor a student and in a school where one would not expect to find such materials being used for research purposes. ... Our concerns were conveyed to the police as the appropriate body to investigate. No judgment was made by us. ... Much has been said on the matter of academic freedom, most of it careless, entirely false and bearing little relation to the facts.'"

He finished. "Not bad," he reacted. "Though if something is *entirely* false it bears *no* relation to the facts, not *little* relation to the facts. And it's perhaps somewhat legalistic, a tad lacking in acknowledgment that things have turned out a bit messy."

"Ah, criticism! Now I know where I am."

"No, no, it's accurate all the same. You will be aware that we – I mean Redman and me – are not used to a Vice Chancellor who takes good advice and tells the truth. I'm not sure the truth is going to do much good in these circumstances, but there's no other way."

"When I saw the VC yesterday he was more concerned to tie this thing up and conclude it and not allow it to survive until President Trump's visit."

"Good luck with that," said McNamara ruefully. "But was he able to tell you any more about China? What exactly are we doing there?"

"Well, everything is difficult and touchy with China now, after last term." Drusilla looked at her watch. "He'll still be with the Minister now, especially if it's something, which I gather it is, that the Minister is not going to like. All I know is that we'll be briefed on Sunday, that you – well, both of us actually, but you will obviously do the talking – have a meeting with Mr Ching on Monday, I shall issue a press release later that day, and we shall remain for the rest of the week dealing with the plentiful coverage that it is anticipated will be the consequence. It seems to be important that we speak from China rather than come back to the Odium immediately."

"Mr *Ching*?" he said.

"Ah, yes. Mr Ching is the person who essentially makes all the major decisions with respect to the China campus."

"But the Provost is someone from here, no? He's not Chinese."

"Professor Miles Dudd, yes. But he's not really in charge, of course. Mr Ching is the Chair of the Chongqing City Communist Party – CCCP for short, ha ha. It adds to the confusion that his other name is Chong and he is thus Chong Ching of Chongqing, but he seems to think this suggests that he was destined by fate for the position in the Party he now occupies. His office seemed impressed when we sent your CV yesterday afternoon. They have never done business with an actual Marxist from Odium. I'm not sure they even knew we had one."

"Oh," said McNamara, feeling a dim light starting to dawn. "Is that why I have been deemed suitable for this task, Drusilla? I might smooth over the enormous faultlines that have opened up between us and the Chinese by means of a little knowledgeable table talk about the materialist dialectic and surplus value?"

"Would one not send a Catholic to meet the Pope if one had a choice?"

"Let's hope he doesn't actually read any of my

publications that mention China. They say it was not a Marxist economy or polity at any stage, even in 1949, never mind later."

"Oh, Mr Ching won't do that. He doesn't speak English, and as far as I can tell he's no intellectual, just a Party functionary. But he will want his picture in all the papers with a prestigious Western Communist."

"I'm not a Communist, Drusilla."

"I think that may get lost in translation," she replied wryly.

"Christ," he muttered. "I suppose I need to accustom myself to this grotesque pantomime."

"It sounds like pantomime," said Lorraine, pouring another gin and tonic for them both.

"That about sums it up," answered Redman. "Not helped by the police transferring Yunus to a detention centre in the morning, so that he could freely use his phone. They were wiser with Faraj. Apparently they didn't let him go 'til after the rally."

"He's out?"

"Well, of course. He didn't do anything criminal. But it's turned into something like an Ealing comedy. Two guys twatting about has become an internationally reported human rights incident, and now that Faraj is liberated you can bet the rhetoric will soar into stratospheric realms of nonsense about how truly oppressed he is. We'll be hearing all about wrongful arrests, despite the fact that both arrests were perfectly legal. We'll have speeches about racism, even though the one remaining issue is no less mundane than the fact that Yunus has committed a petty criminal offence by acquiring a fake stamp in his passport. There will be endless gnashing of teeth about academic freedom, despite the fact that neither of them has such a freedom because neither of them is an academic. Yunus's detention centre will be described as if it's something out of Solzhenitsyn. In short, prepare yourself for all sorts of fiction, poetry and drama, because the real story is too drably administrative and routine for anyone at the demo now to accept, given all the energy and effort they've put into believing the hype. Yunus and Faraj should really be in advertising, because in the last week they've convinced greater minds than theirs that a crock of shit is actually a pot of gold. And we are all going to pay the price."

"Not me," said Lorraine. "I'll stay away if it's going to get worse. In fact, I think I'll send an email to Matthews saying that right now, and ruin his weekend."

"What with the death threats and all," Redman grinned, "I think you could be looking at unchallenged weeks or months off."

"Maybe," said Lorraine. "But I might simply start looking for another job. I used to work in a primary school and, to be frank, it wasn't a place where I had to suffer such lies, cowardice and skulduggery."

Redman nodded.

"Or, to be even more honest," she added, "such stupidity."

Chapter Nine

Enter a man in a white suit which never showed a stain. His name was William Stoner.

The fabric of his unvarying apparel did not remain pristine miraculously, as if in divine outward indication of his moral flawlessness (although he *was* flawless in many more dimensions than the merely ethical), or because it was made of a new synthetic chemical compound, but because he always had ten identical white suits, was (without seeming to be an untouchable) naturally careful what he stood near and where he sat and whom he brushed up against, and had an uncommonly conscientious dry cleaner. If, on private inspection, any of his all-silk ensembles bore a blemish that proved inerasable, he immediately gave the garments to Oxfam.

Stoner did not personally believe that one's outward phenomenon in the world indicated a great deal about one's inner being, but he knew that most other people resolutely did believe that, and that they generally seemed greatly impressed in their dealings with those who maintained high standards of dress. As such an insight demonstrates, he had an enviable understanding of the needs of others: indeed, his being quite free of egoism or vanity, it might plausibly be argued that he dressed selflessly, essentially *for* others, as a kind of impeccable example of *how to be*. Something about the whiteness of his clothes, he came to know, suggested that he was a flag or even a dove of peace. He considered himself nothing of the kind, but like most super-intelligent people was all too aware of being read like a Barthesian myth, and of the seeming advantage (to the world, not to himself) of his being so interpreted. Were he to meet himself as a character in a novel, he knew, his own disbelief would have difficulty in remaining suspended; but in the real world of Odium, where disbelief was a universally required ability for survival, he was taken seriously as a kind of human touchstone of the absolutely civilising qualities of learnedness.

What Stoner did believe in, it possibly goes without saying, were values just like those: for example, that knowledge was the Holy Grail, and that universities existed exclusively to seek it and pass it on. Quite how he ended up at the University of Odium, therefore, is a puzzle requiring explanation.

Stoner was born in north Africa sometime in the nineteen fifties. More than this he never vouchsafed and, oddly, few people asked. It was as if his issuing forth into the world were better comprehended as a continental, rather than a merely national, event. The lack of questions as to his nativity, we may infer, was partly explicable by the accompanying assumptions of a colonial inheritance, the dark details of which might have sullied the spotlessly favourable impression which nearly all his interlocutors had formed of Stoner by the time any mention of his origins may have arisen. Stoner was saved – though his ignorance of the fact actually prevented him in a more profound manner – from ever having to tell anyone that his white unmarried forty-year old father had conceived him upon the conquest of a native farm girl of fourteen, then abandoned her upon hearing of the pregnancy, only to take a renewed interest in him once he popped out of the womb pale white and showing no traces of the expected Moorishness. The father did not go so far as to appropriate the boy as his own son, but chose rather to oversee his fate from afar, and to provide for him, in excess if need be, like a conscience-stricken Dickensian criminal-turned-patron. Stoner never met him. He was packed off to boarding school in England from the age of five, but not before learning the most exquisite Arabic from his young mother, who was not yet twenty.

By the time he went to Oxford, he already spoke English in such a way and had a bearing of such maturity that he was often mistaken for a college fellow, not least because, as he did to this day, he constantly smoked a pipe and smelled permanently like an ashtray. But as he once quipped to McNamara, whom he first met there, he would have preferred to be the college Othello. He had as a youth intended, improbably, to study agriculture, from some feeling in his bones that it would honour his farming mother's increasingly distant memory (she having died in a not-deeply investigated hunting accident on his father's land a mere year after Stoner's departure to England). But in the Bodleian Library's Islamic manuscript collection he found many more compelling ways to keep her in mind.

Since 1602, when it opened, the library had possessed a manuscript of the Quran, which he first held with a kind of awe and then read with increasing understanding and pleasure. The Persian illuminated manuscripts beguiled him. Within a week he had switched to Arabic language and literature (having originally enrolled to study Spanish), which he did by barging into the college rooms of Britain's then greatest living Arabist, and convincing him that his days at pole position were inevitably numbered, and that it would therefore be wise to start training his replacement, who would be him, William Stoner. Like everyone else, the ageing Professor liked Stoner so much at first meeting that he readily agreed upon hearing the young man's fantastic spoken Arabic. When the old man died twenty years later, Stoner was among those who carried his coffin. Everyone present remembered the funeral well, for, while the rest of the congregation was bedecked in black, Stoner chose that moment to assume his evermore permanent public suit of white.

He was never able to replace his mentor at Oxford. While a postgraduate student there, writing the thesis that would prove on publication that there was a really cool new guy in the hot field of pre-Islamic Arabic poetry, Stoner fell in love with, spoke to, impregnated, then married (in that order) a high-born young American woman who had come over on a Fulbright scholarship. Within a year of the birth of their daughter, he found himself teaching in the University of Missouri at Columbia, and living in a splendid town house a few select streets away from his new wife's excessively affluent parents. Unfortunately, his wife turned out to be a manic depressive whose depressive mania had not shown itself in the refined environs of Oxford, where she had fled largely in order to escape the robotic Puritanism of her landowning parents, which had been her depression's primary cause. It displayed itself with a recurring vengeance, predictably, almost as soon as she re-entered their orbit, not least because, in addition to the already long list of things they disapproved of vocally, they disapproved extra-loudly of her ruptured hymen, for whose destruction they mistakenly blamed Stoner. This, in some senses, was a punishment she deserved, for she actively misled them (as she had misled Stoner) as to his culpability for this breach. Her hymen had in fact said hi (and goodbye) to a man long before she had left Missouri for Oxford.

Oxford was one of the few places on earth where someone like Stoner would not seem too unusual, and where to be married to him might feel like an advantage to a woman so emotionally constituted. But in Columbia his odd singularity (and the fact that her parents loathed him) came to feel like a social stigma. His daughter, moreover, looked like him, but not the mother, another fact her parents resented. They proved to be solicitous grandparents, spending much time with their new grand-daughter. The consequence was that, along with her grandparents and her mother, she became one of only five people in the world who ever found it in their hearts to despise Stoner. Stoner knew she had loved him as a little child, but her sensibilities, increasingly manipulated by his wife and her parents, were gradually turned against him. The other person who hated him was an unusually misanthropic colleague at Columbia called Lomax, who tried his best from early acquaintance to damage Stoner's career, only to be foiled once every two years or so when Stoner published the latest in his near-biennial, discipline-defining and promotion-bearing monographs. He was a full Professor at Missouri within a decade.

The handful of hatreds originated solely within the hearts of those who bore them rather than being prompted by anything Stoner actually did or was. He remained entirely innocent in his very adult way. Even his eventual – one might say inevitable – infidelity to his wife was conducted in a kind of innocence, or at least with a kind of purity, the purity of a deep and genuine love for a woman willing to requite it, but which Stoner, in a repetition that proved Einstein's definition of insanity wrong, felt once more even before speaking to her. She was English. She was a good deal younger than him. She was an Arabist. She had come over from Oxford on a Fulbright for the sole purpose of having him as her supervisor. Being a smoker herself, she did not mind his carbonised odour. To do justice in describing their candid relation as it burgeoned would demand an entire chapter of a novel, and a battery of Lawrencean literary techniques – from his unique cadences to his idiosyncratic lexis to his organicist tropes – which might draw the unwelcome quasi-critical attentions of Professor Bernard Matthews to any author who attempted it. To be succinct, suffice to say that, at the end of her period of study, Stoner eloped with her to England. He repatriated himself. As soon as she could, his wife divorced him, and he married the woman he loved and who loved him back. The remainder of life was generally once more beatific to him, because he had dealt with hatred in the best way it can be dealt with: he had walked away from it. He could have written a self-help book on achieving happiness through goodness and patience, had his vocabulary been down to it.

But Oxford was closed to him. He was simply too good. None of the incumbent Arabists wanted him queering their pitch. McNamara, who was now at Odium but not yet in the trough of his own alienation from it, persuaded the University to establish an Institute for Arabic Studies, and to offer Stoner the headship. For a time, Stoner ran the small unit in the time-honoured traditional way, as a research centre of some excellence. But when Sir Evan Covet arrived, he took a dim view of the teaching of an ancient literature largely about deserts, men and camels, and so reconfigured it to his and the contemporary market's pleasing that Stoner opted, without confronting Covet, to take a permanent back seat. Ten years further on, it had become the Department of Arabic Studies, but by far the greatest source of its income was the contribution it made to McNamara's School's popular postgraduate degrees in counter-terrorism, by means of which it provided linguistic training to young people avid for careers in various international security services, principally American and European.

Stoner was a familiar figure on the Odium campus in his twilight years, often walking with what seemed an exaggerated swagger, his right hand usually clutching the bowl of his pipe, smoke billowing from him as if he were a steam train moving at very slow speed. The distinctive gait people attributed to his presumed colonial privileges, or imagined was a sign of his Oxonian-bred self-confidence, but in fact he had picked it up by osmosis in Missouri, where most people were so fat that they had to adopt a swagger in order to be able to lug their hips around at all. Everyone found him charming and inoffensive, though not because he lacked bite or acidity. Once, at a dinner held to mark the presence of academic visitors from Barcelona, he had in the middle of an impromptu speech made a remark about bloody Catalans and their constant snivelling and whining for independence. It was not said in jest, yet everyone assumed that it was, and all laughed at the mischief-making of the mega-erudite rapscallion.

All of Stoner's attempts to make an opinionated mark

on the world tended to end this way. No one took him seriously but, instead, concluded that he had a wickedly teasing sense of humour. Eventually, he abandoned these insidious intents to disturb the universe, and simply watched the smoke that rose from his pipe, realising that the greatness of his moment had already flickered, that he had settled into the status of something like an institutional treasure. Above all he decided never to force any moment to a crisis, but to be deferential, politic, cautious, even if at times it made him, with his famously vast and capacious mind, seem almost ridiculous. As he grew old, this calculated reserve made him appear to others even more monumentally Eliotic than he was. The permanent white suit seemed the perfect apparel for a man whom everybody loved and cherished, but hardly anyone listened to.

As Redman was walking away from the Saturday rally in disgust, he encountered Stoner. The older man had been standing a little further back up the hill, watching the event, just as Redman had been doing.

Stoner took his pipe out of his mouth and greeted him. "I didn't know it was you 'til you turned around, James. I'm not sure why I came here, but I felt I had to. It's a sorry spectacle."

"Yes," said Redman, "and one founded on conscious lying."

"I know," Stoner agreed. "The young man, Yunus, he gave me to believe, when he said he worked in your School, that he was a lecturer there. It's only as a result of this brouhaha and all the press coverage that I discover he's an administrator. Now, he never actually *said* that he was an academic, but the fact that he left the truth *unsaid* throughout all our discussions was, I have come to conclude, deliberately misleading. I never checked because, well, I just never thought it was a deception anyone would try to get away with. You'd know you'd be found out in the end. To his credit, he has enough encyclopaedic knowledge to be able to pass himself off."

"I didn't know you knew him personally."

"I've been meeting him about three times a week for the last year, in the afternoons. We speak Arabic together. He's very well informed about Arab current affairs, you know, and widely read. He teaches me things."

"Ah," said Redman. "That perhaps partly explains his absences during normal work hours. As for the lying about being a lecturer, he's going to keep trying to give that impression. You heard his speech there, yes? 'Fellow members of the academic community' were his actual words, I think."

"It's a shame," Stoner puffed, "that a young, intelligent, promising life should allow itself to drown in lies like that."

"It's a shame that he's causing so much trouble for everyone else by those lies."

"That's true too," said Stoner, "but you know, most of those people down there, the students and the staff, they are the stupidest arseholes of this place, its worst, not its best. There are twenty thousand students in the University altogether. The few hundred down there are just the brainless scum. That Scotsman, for example, Donald Doyle, is it? Have you ever seen such an obviously ignoble creature, someone so perceptibly to be avoided after just a single glance at him? Yet they applaud him. Someone or other would be using them, they'd be believing this arrant nonsense or that utter bilge. The puzzle is how Yunus can associate with them, even in this disembodied telephonic manner, or rather how he can cater to them with that ridiculous speech."

"It's been a verbally violent campaign," said Redman. "It so happens that it's the stupid, or the gullible, who are offering to ride to his rescue. He's persuaded himself to throw his lot in with them because, well, they seem his best chance. I wouldn't be surprised if he thinks that their campaign might actually succeed in freeing him, it's been so vocal and loud."

"But that's the basest of self-deception," said Stoner. "I consider him too intelligent for that. He's not thinking straight."

They heard distant roars and cheers from the assembly down below.

"And the reason he's not thinking straight," Stoner went on, "is that all he can hear these days is the noise of that rabble, drowning out all sense. He does not yet understand that all salvation is founded upon an eventual embrace of the truth, no matter how humbling. I don't think this is because of a defect in his own intelligence. I think it's inexperience."

"I disagree," said Redman. "I think it's vanity."

They stood for a moment in silence, watching the crowd, Stoner savouring his pipe. "Well," he said, "we shall find out."

Stoner went to visit Yunus in the detention centre the next afternoon. It was in Lincolnshire, near Spalding. He was expecting something rather prison-like, and there was a barbed wire fence marking a distant perimeter, and no other significant buildings around it. But the building itself and its innards more resembled a university Hall of Residence. Inmates (so said the brochure in the waiting room) had their own private en suite rooms. It had a common room, a games room, a TV room, a dining room, and a library. The visiting room had partitioned booths. It was clean. Stoner did not fear for the whiteness of his trousers as he sat and waited.

Yunus did not appear for a while and when he did he was smiling broadly. As he put his arms round Stoner he said, in Arabic, "Sorry, I was talking to CNN."

"Yes," said Stoner, returning his Arabic. "I heard you on the radio on *The World This Weekend* as I was driving across in the car. 'Kafkaesque'? You really think this place is Kafkaesque?"

"Oh yeah," said Yunus. "Worse."

"But," said Stoner, "they have told you what crime you have allegedly committed, no?"

"Well, yes," admitted Yunus.

"And it's all been dealt with, so far, within one week? And you have a preliminary court date in another week? So they are processing the case relatively quickly, keeping you informed of it, letting you see your lawyer and visitors, yes?"

"I don't think speed or efficiency has anything to do with it. It's more the manner in which they treat you."

"I see," said Stoner. "You know that in *The Trial* Joseph K. is kept dangling and never knows what he is being charged with and is eventually killed 'like a dog'?"

"I never got to the end of it, to be honest."

"I suppose what I am saying is that these analogies you imagine perhaps make it less rather than more easy for you to cope with the short period of detention, they perhaps encourage you to look at it less stoically and, in fact, to suffer more than is necessary. Take the idea that you have experienced something like Gestapo treatment from the immigration people. I mean, you have not been tortured at all, have you?"

"No, but, as I say, it's more their mentality."

"You mean they think like the Gestapo but don't act like the Gestapo? I presume this thinking of theirs reveals itself in some actions, though?"

"They mainly ignore you. They treat you as if you are not fully human."

"By leaving you alone most of the time? Is that all? But they have explained why you are being detained and why you are going to court. The stamp in the passport, right?"

"Yeah, right."

"And it is an illegal stamp, Yunus, is it not? You paid to have it forged, correct? You know that they are in the right?"

"I'll address that issue in court."

"No doubt. But we are private and confidential here. You and I have always spoken openly and freely. We have often spoken of the value of personal integrity. What will you say in court?"

"I'll say that the stamp is genuine."

"As I understand it, the problem is that that particular stamp was not in use by the immigration services on the date it bears. It had been discontinued a couple of years before. So you could not possibly have got it legitimately."

There was silence. Yunus had stopped smiling. "You come here, I agree to see you, I thought you were my friend. I thought you wanted to help."

"In what way?"

"With the campaign."

"Actually, I came simply to see you. I did not intend to discuss the campaign, which is a sideshow, but just to reassure myself that you were in reasonable spirits. I can see that you are actually in *high* spirits, the finest of fettles. But the campaign does not seem to be about your immigration status, Yunus, which is the one matter now outstanding, given that you and Faraj have been freed without charge on the terrorism counts. The only reason you are in here is that you have a forged stamp in your passport and are an illegal immigrant."

"It's a stitch-up," protested Yunus.

"Now, now, I don't think so," said Stoner. "After all, Yunus, it wouldn't be the first time, would it? You did deliberately give me the misleading impression that you were an academic staff member, and you have done nothing to disabuse me of that impression for the last year. In fact, you have only a second-class degree in Business Administration from the University of Jendouba. Not that this matters to me or says anything about your actual self. You are a deeply intelligent young man and I am sure, if you had had the luck to study something you love, like literature or philosophy, that you could have been an academic. But there is an element of deception in your behaviour, of wishing to be seen as something more exalted than what you are. And I worry that perhaps the excitement of being at the centre of a campaign is having the effect of an adulatory distraction from the fact that, if you go to court, you will be found guilty and probably deported or, worse, sent to prison then deported."

"I'm confident about my case."

Stoner shook his head. "That is impossible, Yunus. I think you are prepossessed with something else."

"What do you mean?"

"It may appear to you – you're on the BBC and in the newspapers every day – that you are the eye of some epoch-making storm, politically profound, heroic, even. The media have fallen for the 'academic freedom' blather because it makes for a good story. But the truth is, you are attempting to keep an issue alive which is procedurally dead. The only live issue is now your immigration status, and that has nothing to do with the University of Odium, indeed they were witless enough to take your word for it. But you seem to want to promote the idea to the world that you are blameless and that you ended up here because of a gutless university and an oppressive government. In fact, you are here because you bribed someone to forge a passport stamp, and that person didn't do it very well."

"With all these people behind me, I'll win my case."

"But they are not behind you in your case, Yunus. They are behind the straw monster of violated academic freedom, which never even happened. They hear you say that you are innocent of the illegal immigration charge, and so they are persuaded, because you precisely try so to persuade them, that it is a trumped-up police trick in order to punish you for something much more politically serious. But you and I and anyone who thinks knows that your case is in fact glamourless and dispiritingly everyday. If you are found guilty, and go to jail, I imagine you can delude yourself that you will be a political prisoner, but let's get real. You'll serve six months and then they will stick you on a plane back home to Tunisia, that great land of freedom, democracy and human rights. Who wants that?"

Yunus now seemed to be simmering with anger, but he contained himself. "And what do you suggest as an alternative?"

"Proceed from the truth. Call off this ridiculous academic freedom campaign you are waging against your ex-employer. If you do that, plenty of people in the University will offer themselves as character witnesses for you. Nobody in the University has any interest in seeing you behind bars, but you have done nothing but calumniate them for the last seven days, so no one who matters now feels like helping you. Admit to the illegal action. You might get a suspended sentence. It might help should you make an application to remain in the country thereafter. It might forestall a deportation. But the most important thing of all is to acknowledge the truth and not to perjure yourself."

Yunus stood up. He did not offer to embrace Stoner this time, but held out a hand, and took the older man's and shook it without much enthusiasm.

"I wish I could thank you for coming to see me," he said, with a formality which seemed now to be the only thing repressing his self-righteous indignation. "But we fundamentally disagree. You overrate the truth. It has only a small place in politics. Politics is all about opportunity, and a truly political person does not shirk an opportunity like this when it arises, because it is not just about him, but about all those on whose behalf he seizes it."

Stoner understood that he was something worse than no longer welcome: the main thing now was that he was no longer *useful*. "Then you really are in something like Kafka's *The Trial*," he said as he paused before finally leaving the place. "You're in a fiction of your own authorship."

Stoner had to drive into Spalding on the way home, looking for somewhere that sold pipe tobacco. It being late on a Sunday afternoon, this was not a straightforward task. Everywhere was closed on the approach to the town, which seemed sedgy and overgrown, as if the local council had no money to manicure the place with any regularity. House after house with off-white or brown porridgy rendering slid past. These finally gave way to a warren of tarmac and brick streets around the town square, which in fact appeared to be more of a town triangle, its ageing architecture not unpleasant, but dirty and crumbling, down at heel. The Lincolnshire landscape and the soulless small-town streets reminded him of Missouri, except Missouri was better looking.

He found an open petrol station near the centre and made his purchase. As he returned to his car, which he had parked in a side street, he saw that he had left it in the shadow of a great dark warehouse-type building. It was constructed of corrugated metal, which had turned mottled grey in years of weather. Along the top, to admit light, was an entire row of windows, every one of which had been shattered, presumably by stones thrown upward from the pavement with deliberate intent. The seemingly bombed-out structure was surrounded by cracked and weedy paving slabs, and lent a grim mood to the row of ragged houses at whose end it squatted.

He walked past his car to the end of the building and, looking up, saw that it had been a postal sorting office. He remembered that the Royal Mail had been privatised three or four years before. This must have been the consequence for Spalding, and no going concern had stepped in to give the unremarkable edifice a continued role in the economy of the town. A brief image of the alabaster-white Trump Building flared up in his imagination, as if to suggest a deliberate contrast. Its concerns, and his concerns with its concerns, seemed a sudden extravagance in a world in which 'academic freedom' and even 'freedom of speech' must be of trivial moment compared to the imperious need to work and earn. He was fleetingly disgusted by the rhetoric of his own comparatively pampered profession and class. Yet poor Spalding, in the fifth richest country on the globe, was still a haven compared to the townships of the north

African land of his birth. What was talk of freedom or self-integrity worth in a world thoroughly governed still by need? He sat in the car morosely, smoking his pipe with the window open. He finally drove off with a sigh and a shake of the head.

He turned on CNN straight away when he got home. He then went into a bedroom to change.

After a few minutes the Yunus segment was played. Stoner came into the living room in his shirt, underwear and socks, and stood to watch it. It was a recording of a telephone interview, accompanied by a still photo of Yunus. Under it were given his name and, misleadingly, the words "University of Odium, UK". Stoner heard Yunus claim that his re-arrest most likely would not have happened were it not for the initial political context of the first arrests, that the authorities had been draconian in their actions and that this was clearly their attempt to try and "cover up the initial mistake". This was expressed with great media fluency, which only increased Stoner's sense of unease.

He called Redman. There was no answer, so he left a short message: "Hello, James. Stoner here. I saw Yunus. You were right and I was wrong. He is indeed a case of overreaching self-conceit. Ciao."

Afterwards, reflexively, he went into the bedroom and examined the suit he had been wearing that day, which he had spread out on the top of the bed.

He gave it very close scrutiny. But it bore no stain.

Chapter Ten

McNamara had never been to Chongqing before. But he had visited Ningbo, where the first ever British university campus had been set up twelve years before, and where he had witnessed, to his horror, an unimaginably miserable franchise operation with Nuremberg architecture and students who could speak hardly any English. He had encountered a young female student there one day who was not Chinese but had come from Denmark on a one-semester exchange visit. She was a sociologist. But in Ningbo, which hardly had a Social Sciences faculty to speak of, she was forced to take modules from a degree course in a pseudo-subject called International Communications. He asked her what she thought of the course. She immediately erupted in a flood of tears. "It's terrible," she had said. "Everything here is terrible. It's the biggest mistake I ever made, coming here." He had agreed with her silently. Even after he left, he felt contaminated by the Chinese conception of a university and, most of all, the abject British willingness to cater to it.

Chongqing is a city much further west than the near-coastal Ningbo, which is usually a bad sign in China, the interior being generally less developed and much poorer.

But in fact he had found little difference in his admittedly brief impressions so far. He was shocked, virtually before he had left the airport, to witness the dreadful local manners, which he realised he had noticed on his last trip but must quickly have forgotten. Drusilla, whom on the outward journey he had begun to appreciate as a woman with a decent sense of style, had been to China many more times than him, and did not, as he had thought she might, immediately curl up and die. In fact, she seemed to have learned a fair amount of transactional Chinese, and to be professionally inured to the host of indignities one regularly had to see, avoid, or actually suffer: people bumping into you and not murmuring even the slightest apology, failing also on every occasion to hold doors open for anyone following; if you arrived at a gate and there was someone on the other side, they just pushed through, and even if you held it open for them they did not say thank you; queue-jumping seemed universal; no matter what you said to a taxi driver, his first utterance was a very loud question that sounded like "Samah?", simply because they were white and he therefore assumed he could not possibly understand Drusilla's Chinese; even female taxi drivers, of which there were a few, did this and likewise sounded like snarling dogs, usually with two or three teeth missing. Everyone appeared to dress in cheap fabrics, like chiffon, with styles that had not been seen in the West since the nineteen-seventies. The men in particular often had a slack-jawed look, and almost all of them smoked, even in tiny elevators with signs which prohibited it; the women sported whacky hairdos and big ugly glasses and sat with their legs spread wide in public places, happily burping loud and long after eating. When they spoke into their mobile phones the Chinese often shouted (because the person they are talking to is far away, Drusilla explained, or, as she actually put it, "they think they are still in the paddy field"); men spat all the time, great gobs of grey-green everywhere, even sometimes on the floors of restaurants, most of which were insufferably noisy because they were full of sounds which simply did sound like high-pitched human squawking; an order to a waitress would result in her turning around and bellowing your wishes down the restaurant to the person at the counter; if you walked past this same restaurant at four in the afternoon, you would see the same waitress with her head on the table in an entire row of tables with similarly sleeping girls: they would all be getting some shut-eye until the evening shift began. Most restaurants were of dubious hygiene, which perhaps explained the rampant success of the many sprouting and comparatively antiseptic branches of McDonalds and KFC and Starbucks.

Drusilla had impressed him by pointing out that, despite much of it having been planned in the last decade, Chongqing was an utter disaster from the point of view of all modern design. For example, there were hardly any ramps anywhere, and pavements were sometimes as much as nine inches or a foot above the road. Drains were often open; had it been summer, the streets would have stunk. Many public objects were placed at a height which guaranteed that human heads would crash into them. Every twenty yards or so a lamppost arose from the very middle of a pavement, making it impossible for pushchairs or wheelchairs to pass. It was as if the architecture had been demonically conceived deliberately to cause the maximum quantum of harm and inconvenience rather than the reverse.

In short, by the end even of their first shared meal on the Sunday evening they arrived, McNamara and Drusilla had begun to form a strong emotional bond founded on the shared racism and intolerance which seemed spontaneously to ignite within them when confronted with anything natively Chinese. Indeed, they began to enjoy the feeling of defending themselves and each other against the frequent assaults to their senses and sensibilities. When the empirical evidence presented directly to them seemed exhausted, they began to seek out less obvious cultural abominations and provocations to confirm them in their negative responses.

Although McNamara had heard that the Chongqing campus was owned by the same "educational company" as the Ningbo campus, and that it was in every architectural respect indistinguishable from it, he had considered this claim to be improbable, exaggerated. But in fact it was quite true. There was the same administration block with a clock tower, whose same chimes were in fact the same MP3 recording piped through a loudspeaker, with a road as wide as a motorway stretching out from it for a quarter of a mile, ending in three mammoth ugly white teaching blocks, behind which was exactly the same array of student residences as were to be found in Ningbo. The Ningbo campus had been *exactly* recreated in Chongqing, in the same way that urban planners reproduce the same tower blocks in different sectors of Chinese cities. The University Hotel, where he and Drusilla were put up, had the same number of floors, and rooms, and an identical internal layout.

The food in its foyer restaurant was tolerable; what it called coffee was inferior in taste to greasy dishwater. They opted for alcohol instead. While Drusilla was ordering, McNamara slipped away to his room to make a scheduled phone call to the Vice Chancellor. When he returned his face bore a rather different and startled expression, one that seemed a little prompted by a rush of adrenalin, as if he had opened the door on a room in which he expected to be welcomed by a puppy and instead had encountered a wolf. He sat once more opposite her and began to toy with his glass of red wine.

"Well?" said Drusilla.

"Not exactly what I was anticipating. Let me ask you, Drusilla, in what kind of detail were you briefed before coming out here?"

"As much or less than you," she replied. "The VC had a meeting with the Minister on Saturday; it was likely to be a difficult one, he said; he would instruct us on the actions to be taken as a consequence once we arrived here. I got the sense that he knew what he wanted to do but that quite how we would do it or whether we would be able to do it depended on that meeting."

"He didn't actually say what he wanted to do?"

"No. But I assume he has now told you?"

McNamara nodded. "You have a sealed letter, apparently? Spooner will entrust nothing to email about this. He reckons the authorities have access to all our China-based servers."

"Oh, yes," said Drusilla. "The VC gave me a letter. He said we would probably need it and he would tell me when to present it. It's for Mr Ching."

"You don't know its contents?" said McNamara.

"It's in Chinese," said Drusilla.

McNamara drank a little.

"Well," he said, "it's apparently a two-sentence letter telling Mr Ching that the University of Odium will be taking no more students and shall withdraw from China when the last cohort of its current students in Chongqing graduates. In other words, we're closing down the operation in four and a half years, little more than a decade after we opened it. I gather this is going to come as a shock to Mr Ching."

Drusilla's eyes had widened. "But not to you?" she said.

"Oh, yes," said McNamara, "I've just had time to get used to the idea as I was coming back downstairs. I wouldn't quite believe it unless the VC had told me himself. Apparently the Minister back in London is livid."

"I can imagine. She's ethnically Chinese herself. Educational cooperation is a likely plank of any independent trade agreement we make with China after Brexit. Anything that threatens such cooperation weakens the British hand."

"According to Spooner, he told her flatly that he held her personally to blame, that her attempts to shaft us last term over Odiumgate had been a deciding factor for him, and not just the grief the Chinese have given us ever since. If the Chongqing connection was going to be used to blackmail us, he informed her, the University Council would rather not maintain it."

"I'm surprised he managed to get the Council's backing, and, to think of it, to prevent anyone leaking the decision. I usually find out about such leaks quite quickly: it's me the media call."

"The Council is still a skeleton crew these days. After all the resignations of last term, it's down to half its normally operating numbers, and local worthies are more circumspect about signing up. Plus the VC deliberately didn't hold the Council meeting 'til Friday afternoon. So there's been little time for any leaking to be done."

"Should we be celebrating?" Drusilla lifted her glass. She was beginning to enjoy herself. "I hate this place and I hate coming here. If this is the last time..."

McNamara reciprocated. "Yes, I think we should. We should never have been here. It was an appalling decision made for all the wrong reasons, principally so that Sir Evan Covet could get his knighthood, I understand. From the point of view of academic standards, it's been utterly ruinous. We've been dishing out Odium degrees like lollipops to Chinese students who simply wouldn't be admitted if they applied for entry in the UK. It's debased our coinage."

They clinked glasses and drank.

"The VC," McNamara continued, "gave some very specific instructions for the delivery of the letter and what we should do thereafter. One, there should be no parley or negotiation with Mr Ching. We refuse all offers of hospitality, deliver the letter, wait 'til he has read it, and leave immediately. Then we get out of town, go to Shanghai, and await the inevitable storm."

"More media outlets in Shanghai," she explained, "including Western ones. But why are we to be so rude when we deliver the letter?"

McNamara inclined his head in open acknowledgment of admiration. "I have to hand it to Spooner, he doesn't do things by halves. He is hoping that the Chinese will be so incensed that they won't accept the four-and-a-half-year wind-down period. If we can provoke them into being all macho and thoughtless, which is how they usually are, he's hoping they will take the huff and shut down the Chongqing operation *immediately*, at the end of this academic year. They'll transfer the students to other Chinese universities. Or they can simply take it over lock, stock and barrel. This being a totalitarian dictatorship, they can do that."

Drusilla asked, "But the non-Chinese students, what about them?"

"Transfer to Odium, all fees waived, for the remainder of their degree courses. It's like depriving them of a tent and replacing it with a villa. So not a big deal, or rather, a very good deal, for them. There are only slightly more than four hundred international students here. That problem can be solved in one stroke."

"So," Drusilla mused, "we are about to become public enemies numbers one and two in the Chinese press for the next few days."

"If we play our cards right," he said, offering another playful toast.

McNamara and Drusilla met Mr Ching the next morning in an opulent penthouse office accessed by a private elevator placed outside the somewhat more ordinary administrative quarters of the campus Provost, Professor Miles Dudd.

Dudd was a thin, silver-haired Dubliner, an art historian who had published one or two slim volumes on negligible Irish painting, which he considered reason sufficient to describe himself as a "writer" on his Wikipedia page. There was no Art History department on the Chongqing campus, of course: Dudd had been seconded to the job two months ago because no one else of professorial standing had been incautious enough to put themselves forward after the recall of his predecessor in the wake of the diplomatic rift which had erupted between Odium and the Chinese government. A contributory factor was that his departmental colleagues back in Odium were fervent in their encouragement that he should go.

McNamara knew Dudd as a beaming impostor, the kind of man who sees so little beyond his own diminutive ego that truly significant events pass him by without his noticing. He asked Dudd how things were going and the latter replied breezily, "Great! I see it as my role to let things happen!" At this smug and ridiculous statement, which Dudd emitted as if it were a *pensée* of Pascalian order, McNamara decided that he would accordingly make what was about to happen take place without giving Dudd any warning. He let the Irishman escort them to the accompanying elevator in a practised staccato strut McNamara recognised as part of the simulacrum of flaunted power. Dudd had obviously fallen in love with the external trappings of the office: the chauffeur, the handful of flunkies, the house on the island in the artificial lake, the six-figure salary, the endless opportunities to speak in the imperative. When he had been at Odium, he had been a lolloper, head down and shoulders always sagging, slow of pace. Now he looked as if he were about to marshal squaddies on a parade ground.

Ching and Dudd appeared to be temperamentally suited to one another. The Chinese man had glossy cheeks, the stature of a Napoleon, was bow-legged, jaunty in his gait, bore a smile that was too broad to be anything but patronising, and he made disconcerting little grunts and gasps when he was not speaking, as if there were a tiny gremlin always busily at work in the olfactory bulb at the back of his nose. In other words, like nearly all local Chinese Communist Party bigwigs, he was a repellent little toad who listened to no one, or at least to no one in Chongqing. He greeted them with sweeping gestures of both arms and a booming, throaty, obviously prepared piece of rhetoric, in Chinese.

His P.A., a demure and rather cowed woman in her thirties whom Ching introduced as Meifeng, bowed a little and translated instantly. Evidently she came from one of the parts of China where the phonemes represented by the letters *r* and *l* are not reversed in pronunciation, or she had been well educated. Her English was faultless. "Mr Ching welcomes the new Pro-Vice Chancellor of the University of Odium to Chongqing! He would like to convey the honour he feels to be meeting such a prestigious Marxist thinker!"

"Thank you," said McNamara.

Mr Ching beckoned for them to sit on a low couch and turned to make the short journey to the much higher seating position he wished to occupy on the far side of his desk. Dudd readily acquiesced and relaxed into the soft leather, but when Ching settled back into his chair he discovered that McNamara still loomed over him, his barrel shape somewhat intimidating, and that Drusilla had not accepted the invitation to sit either. She was standing at his side.

"I have a letter for you," said McNamara, "from Vice Chancellor Spooner. This is the only business we have to conduct today."

McNamara put the sealed envelope on the desk while the translator Chinesed his words uneasily. Ching's smile narrowed from four inches wide across his face to about three and a half, though it still remained imprinted there. He wafted a hand in the direction of the reclining Dudd.

"Mr Ching would be grateful if you would be seated," said Meifeng. It was clearly part of her role to verbalise physical gestures as well as translate articulated sounds, even when this was not strictly necessary. She appeared agitated.

"Thank you," said McNamara, "but no. We will stay for a few minutes if he wishes to read the letter."

While she explained to Ching, Drusilla looked at Dudd and advised in a low voice, "I'd get up if I were you. We're not staying, and believe me, you won't wish to either."

Dudd had got used to the language of command and instantly recognised it. Without thought or challenge, as if Drusilla were a senior member of the Odium Management Board rather than simply its most senior PR hack, he obeyed.

Ching now looked displeased. He reached for an ostentatious silver letter opener. He read the short missive with his lips moving slowly. When he looked up, his craniometry seemed to have changed. He looked more glabellous. His forehead had furrowed intensely and seemed now suddenly to be protuberant, forming a consternated shelf brooding above his eyes. These same eyes then turned up at McNamara, smaller, needling, narrowed, darker. He rose to his feet slowly, the page trembling in his hand, and said something in a low growl, the tone unmistakably menacing.

There was silence. After a second or two McNamara looked at the translator, who had her eyes aimed at her shoes, and was shaking her head slowly.

"I think," said Drusilla, "he just asked what the blazes, as it were, is going on."

"Okay," said McNamara, "he's got the gist." He held out his hand. "Goodbye, Mr Ching."

Ching ignored the proffered handshake. McNamara turned. Drusilla turned.

"But what the blazes *is* going on?" said Dudd, as he too turned.

"We're leaving," said Drusilla. "I'd come with us, if I were you. I can explain outside."

"I see," said Dudd. "Whatever you say."

They had taken only a few steps towards the door when Ching intercepted them, scurrying on short legs from around his desk and interposing himself between the exit and them. He was clearly in a rising fury, and his voice was still loud and rasping but, as he let off an entire paragraph of what sounded like scurrilous invective, the tone slowly changed, along with the expression on his face, and seemed to admit, towards the end, an element of pleading. At the cessation of his outpouring, McNamara looked to Meifeng. She had begun gazing downwards again halfway through his tirade. Now she slowly turned her face up.

"Cannot," she said to McNamara.

"I understand," he acknowledged. "It is obscene?"

She nodded.

Ching began to reproach the translator directly, jabbing his finger at her, clearly commanding her to translate his words.

"Let's pretend," McNamara suggested to her, "because it does not really matter what he says, not any more. Tell me, where did you study?"

"Thank you," Meifeng said very graciously. "I read English Literature at St Andrew's and then I took a Masters at Durham. I enjoyed my time in Britain very much. I miss my friends there. I hope to come again some time. It would be my dream to work there. This is most awkward."

McNamara smiled a little at her in sympathy. Then he looked at Ching severely and raised his voice and his hand, and to everyone's astonishment, especially Dudd's, he wagged his own index finger in front of Ching's snorting nose in an act of unambiguous physical provocation. "I did not come here to be insulted, Mr Ching!" he bellowed. "Now get out of the way, or I shall have to pick you up and move you aside personally. It's time to say *zàijiàn*."

*

They spent five minutes briefing Dudd, and then they both fled to the airport for the next flight to Shanghai. Drusilla fired off a prepared press release to an enormous email list before they settled into their seats in the first class cabin. Things got even better in Shanghai, where they discovered that they each had been booked in for the rest of the week to their own private suites at the Ritz-Carlton at 8 Century Avenue in the Pudong district. ("Rucky Chinese number!" Drusilla exclaimed.) There was little time to relax that evening, however: the calls started coming in from the UK media, eight hours behind China, almost as soon as they arrived, and McNamara was up all night because he agreed to do a live interview on *Newsnight*. Drusilla met him afterwards in the breakfast room, looking beady-eyed and slow-witted.

"How did it go?" she asked.

"Pretty well," he said. "The British media seem to think it's a good move. The hardest question I got was, why had we ever gone to China in the first place?"

"What did you say?"

"I said it was the vanity project of an ex-Vice Chancellor, part of a general overreaching on his part that ended in the ultimate catastrophe of last term. This seems at least partly true."

"And you can't libel the dead," said Drusilla cheerily.

"Can you believe they got a quote from Donald Trump? They played it just before my interview. He thought it was a great idea, getting the hell out of China. He praised Spooner personally. Said he himself would be looking to American universities to justify their presence in China too, now that NYU is here in Shanghai."

"Wow!" said Drusilla.

"Well, no, if Donald Trump endorses you, I think you should maybe start to get worried."

"It's a bit late for that!" laughed Drusilla. "In PR terms it's brilliant, especially given the Trump money deal. The story begins to look coherent."

"You mean it begins to look coherently right-wing," McNamara rejoined. "Still, I agree we did need to get out of China. It was a fiasco from the first. They asked me near the end of the interview about the other big Odium story of the moment, of course. That was not so good. I had perhaps said too much about the constraints placed on our operation by the Chinese. So they quizzed me about the 'similar lack of academic freedom' back in Odium itself. I think I may have been a bit too forthright. I said the allegations were contemptible and false. I repeated that neither Yunus or Faraj had academic freedom because only academics did."

"That's alright, then, isn't it?"

"I'm not sure. Everyone's up for a bit of China-baiting, they like it when sprats like the British throw a dart in China's whale blubber. But calling a pair of local Muslim boys liars goes down a lot less well. The David-Goliath dynamic seems to get reversed when we do that."

"I mean it's alright *in terms of discharging your functions*. It's alright in that you did not put a foot wrong or go off-message."

"Is that all it's about, Drusilla? Discharging your functions? Doing your little bit? Not questioning the overall wisdom of the direction of travel? Not taking issue with the morality of it all?"

"Yes," she said categorically. "That's what it's always been about at all levels in a modern university. I don't set the agenda. I present it."

"Yes, I understand that, in your case. But senior managers are meant to help set the agenda. Vice Chancellors ultimately fix the agenda. I had nothing to do with this decision, even though I approve of it in principle. I'm beginning to wonder how much it was approved – for just some accountability's sake, not a naïve belief in institutional democracy – by the hardly functioning University Council. From where I am standing it looks as if Spooner largely gerrymandered the decision himself and sent me out to execute it. That's pretty close to the moral equivalent of Covet bringing us out here in the first place. And so part of me wonders how deep he is in with similarly anti-China Trump. The British government didn't want us out of China; the American President was happy about it. Should a British university not pause for serious thought at facts like that?"

"What, even if the American President is giving you money that the British government isn't? Doesn't he who pays the piper call the tune?"

McNamara mulled this over. Drusilla was again correct in a purely technical sense. One of the reasons Whitehall had been unable to stop Spooner withdrawing from China was that it had largely washed its hands of universities' funding years ago and no longer paid for their teaching. As a consequence, it had little to blackmail or bribe Spooner with and little other means of traction with him. It did not fund the meagre research that had been conducted at the Chongqing campus.

"The fundamental moral problem, Drusilla, is that we work in an apparently public sector in which it should not be possible or necessary for the American President to have his thumbs in the scales of a British university."

"I don't see why not," she said feistily. "He can buy Scottish land and turn it into golf courses. It's just the logical outcome of globalisation. The key difference would seem to be that he can't actually *buy* the University of Odium but only donate to it. The only compromise we have to make is be polite and friendly to him while we bank his cash. It doesn't *determine* anything, which is why we are able to devote those funds to an expansion of non-commercial subjects. In fact, if you put what we have just done here in China into the narrative, we ourselves seem to be drawing a line under globalisation. There are limits to what we are prepared to accept in its name. And we are no longer prepared to accept giving away University of Odium degrees for a mess of Chinese pottage."

"It must have crossed your mind," he said, "that the only reason this is so is that we may have traded China for a similar mess of Trump pottage."

"Well, yes," she admitted. "But I repeat, ours is not to reason why."

McNamara went to bed and slept heavily, leaving Drusilla to deal with any daytime press. At around three in the afternoon he was awoken by a loud rapping on the door of his suite. He got up and answered it in his hotel dressing gown.

It was Drusilla. She looked jubilant. She raised both of her arms in the air and shook them in triumph. "Job done!" she exclaimed.

"What do you mean?" he asked blearily.

"The Chinese! They took the bait! They've pulled the plug! They're not prepared to put up with us for another four and a half years. We have to be out by the first of September. They're taking over the Chongqing campus, virtually nationalising it! It's to become a Chinese university! They're triggering the clause that allows them to buy back our holding. We're even making money on the deal!"

McNamara did not know what to think, but was rather swept up in Drusilla's infectious enthusiasm.

"I need a drink!" she whooped, and strolled into his room, heading for the mini-bar.

He did not remember exactly how or when they ended up in bed, though he could not deny that he enjoyed every moment they spent there. Drusilla was in a bewitchingly buoyant mood, she was dressed and made-up to the nines because she had been in front of cameras, she was full of praise for the way he had handled himself in public, all traces of their previous enmity seemed to have been wiped from her memory cells, and drink must have done the rest. The foreplay was long. Congress itself was not brief, but only because it was slow, a bit like sliding gently from a wet mud bank into slimy water, except that Drusilla was warm, warm, and soft, and welcoming, and seemingly as desirous as she was desirable. The afterplay was gentle and drawn-out, peppered by much talking of a personal kind, and more alcohol.

For the rest of the week nothing outside the framing rectangle of their shared bed seemed to have any serious purchase on his existence, even as he dealt with the chores each day threw up. He got to know much about her which he could never have guessed, and to touch her in ways that he had never touched Rachel Brace, the last woman who had surrendered herself to him of her entirely free will. He felt nothing of the sordidness he had experienced in his dreams with the necrotic Jane Blake or her substitute pornographic diva or the ultra-compliant harlot who had superseded both in Amsterdam. What he did feel was perfectly figured in Drusilla's words late in the night before they left, as he came out of the bathroom, and the room was dark, and he heard her softly call his first name.

"Yes?" he said.

"Please make love to me again," she implored.

169

Chapter Eleven

"I'm sorry I didn't reply to your emails last week," McNamara said to Redman. "To be honest, we were so busy I didn't have time to catch up on them until we were in the departure lounge. The Odium Two seemed a little less urgent than the China Syndrome. But now I understand the two have been connected."

They were sitting in McNamara's kitchen. It was Monday morning, barely thirty-six hours since his return from China. He had just finished describing the Chongqing drama to Redman.

"It's a very clever campaign," Redman agreed. "Of course, it was Trump who sparked the flame. The students appear to be opposed to the withdrawal from China: you know, fling a few feel-good words at them, like *internationalism*, stir the slightest brotherhood-of-man feeling into their sensitive brain mush, say nothing at all about the abiding horrors of the Chinese Commie Party, especially its repression of free speech, and they're all yours. So when Trump opens his mouth and approves of the decision publicly, *and he's coming here on Thursday of this week*, well, he's suddenly in the eye of the campaign's souped-up storm. Never mind the grotesque contradictions. The political logic now is, Odium has become a right-wing university because it does not protect freedom of speech, and what other signs are there of this, or why is it so?"

"Become?" said McNamara. "This *is* a right-wing university, always has been in my time here."

"True, but in this caricature its recent financial association with Trump is offered as both confirmation and cause. It's a clever way of ensuring the campaigners have new things to do, stay active. The next protest has been called against Trump's visit, and we can expect that it will be an *invasion*, because thousands will pour in from far and wide to deride The Donald. The Odium Two will massively enhance their fanbase because their lieutenants, including large numbers of deluded staff, will be canvassing it, petitioning their supporters, all day long. And Trump will almost certainly say something inane to assist them."

"But the China decision had nothing to do with Trump."

"You sure?"

McNamara grimaced with incredulity. "You cannot possibly think Spooner was *doing Trump's bidding* in pulling out of China," he snorted. "Why would the President of the United States give a damn?"

"No, of course not," Redman replied. "But it's not about the truth or otherwise of specific claims. It's about smearing things together into a political Pollock canvas that students are persuaded they should like. First of all we have a building given Trump's name. Second, we accept a massive and possibly tax-dodging Trump donation. Third, we become the biggest institution of any note except Google to get out of China, something Trump said he would make American companies do. So you can see why we are now being read as rather Trumpish in our ideological complexion, surely? A mere ten years after promulgating our global expansion, we shrink back to our little home island. It fits right in with the Brexit mood, and let's not forget that Trump approves of Brexit too."

"Ha! Google!" McNamara exclaimed. "They threw in the China towel over censorship issues. How ironic!"

Redman noted the attempt at digression, and ignored it. He decided to make a more personal attempt to elicit an engaged response.

"For example," he said, "when they played the Trump tape on *Newsnight*, and asked you if you agreed with him..."

"What was I meant to say?" McNamara interrupted. "That I think he is an idiot? Trump is about to hand over a truckload of gold. No serious person in my position would put that at risk."

"I agree," Redman relented. "It must have been difficult for you."

"No, in fact!" McNamara expostulated. "As Pro-Vice Chancellor of the University, I stand in for the Vice Chancellor. I don't speak on my own behalf. It's an office. Also, it so happens that *on this matter* Trump finds himself in agreement *with me*. It was me, after all, who delivered the letter. He was the one who was asked if *he* agreed with what *we'd* done. This then gets reverse-mangled by the fucking BBC and I am asked if *I agree with him*! It was the nearly dawn in Shanghai. I wasn't at my most alert."

"You simply said yes," Redman laughed. "Clever interviewer, that Evan Davies. So the University of Odium agrees with Donald Trump."

"That's preposterous!" McNamara scoffed. "What does that even *mean*? The statement simply turns a concrete particular into an abstract universal. It makes it sound as if we agree with all that is Trump, rather than our coincidentally sharing with him the same opinion on a single, small decision."

"And that's exactly how it is playing, as a universal, not a particular" said Redman conclusively. He reached for his iPad. "Let me show you something. It's called a mash-up."

McNamara groaned with disrelish as Redman logged on to the Facebook page of the Odium Two campaign. The two-minute video he showed McNamara consisted largely of a series of loathsome Donald Trump quotations, spoken by the man himself in interviews or speeches, interspliced with the repeated, identical scene from *Newsnight* in which Evan Davies asked McNamara if he agreed with Trump. Various written words and phrases had been edited in and bounced and shuttled across the screen for the duration, in subliminal transparent fonts, like "snake oil" and "misogynist" and "liar". There was also a low, slightly comic jingle sounding in the background. But the verbal soundtrack, with its constructed juxtapositions, created the primary effect:

TRUMP: When Mexico sends its people, they're not sending the best. They're sending people that have lots of problems. They're bringing drugs. They bring crime. They're rapists.

DAVIES: Professor McNamara, do you agree with Donald Trump?

McNAMARA: Yes.

TRUMP: The beauty of me is that I'm very rich.

DAVIES: Professor McNamara, do you agree with Donald Trump?

McNAMARA: Yes.

TRUMP: It's freezing and snowing in New York – we need global warming!

DAVIES: Professor McNamara, do you agree with Donald Trump?

McNAMARA: Yes.

TRUMP: You know, it really doesn't matter what the media write as long as you've got a young, and beautiful, piece of ass.

DAVIES: Professor McNamara, do you agree with Donald Trump?

McNAMARA: Yes.

TRUMP: I'm pleased that the University of Odium is getting out of China. American universities ought to follow their example.

DAVIES: Professor McNamara, do you agree with Donald Trump?

McNAMARA: Yes.

McNamara smiled with faint bemusement. "It's just so childish," he remarked.

"Facebook is where today's youth gets its news," said Redman. "The only thing they know about *Newsnight* is what they see on Facebook or Twitter or YouTube about *Newsnight*. They don't see satire as making fun of politics: they think it is a legitimate way of *conducting* politics. Look how many likes this has."

McNamara squinted at the screen. "Does that say what I think it says? Is that six figures?"

"In one week, yes. If you click through to YouTube, where the video is hosted, the number of watches is in seven figures. This is the biggest audience you've ever had, Robert. This is what you are to them. Trump's yes-man. Just read the comments."

McNamara gestured helplessly at the unaccountable

juvenility of it all. What he really wanted to retort was that it really didn't matter what Facebook or Twitter or YouTube said, because he had a middle-aged but still desirable piece of ass. But he did not think that anyone in the University would want to hear about him and Drusilla just yet, least of all Redman.

Fifteen minutes later they walked together up to the Trump Building. There was an awkward moment as they stopped in the corridor of the west wing, McNamara intending to go right into the Vice Chancellor's suite, Redman hovering before turning left into the Registrar's office opposite. They looked briefly towards each other and their expressions glinted in the humour of the moment, its bejewelled ironies. McNamara nodded with half a smile and made his entrance. Redman went through his appointed door, said hello to Alison Stilt, and proceeded to the inner sanctum. There he found Nigel Asterisk and Drusilla Frost.

"Hello. Have you recovered from China?" he asked Drusilla.

Drusilla replied, "Not quite."

"I spoke to Robert," Redman said.

Drusilla gave a small, studied smile. "He was very firm," she said. "With the Chinese, I mean."

"You got on?" Redman appeared interested.

"Well, what did he say?" she rejoined brightly.

"He was extremely complimentary about you. Despite the task you both had, he seemed to enjoy it."

"Me too," she said. "And Professor McNamara was charming."

Asterisk interrupted. "We were just saying, it's like we're having a streak of good luck. Actually to be making money on the China deal is nothing short of a miracle. It's played well in the press, if not with the home students. To be shot of the entire thing by the first of September is just Dreamsville. But as one door closes a different trap door might open, if we don't manage Thursday with some deftness."

"I expect," Redman said, "that Thursday will be a political nightmare, not to say a massive security risk. Deftness has never been our stock-in-trade. We might try to find out what the Union is up to."

"How?" asked Asterisk.

"Robert is with the VC now. He's going to suggest that we drop in on Avril Poon."

"You and PVC McNamara? Before Thursday?"

"Right now, today," Redman confirmed.

"But why would the Union president share any information? The Union is against us on this. It's anti-Trump and pro-Odium Two."

"Not to mention being suddenly pro-China," Drusilla sighed. She was making to leave.

Redman smiled wryly. "You never know. We might be able to persuade her by, er, leaning on old loyalties. In any case, the VC will decide. You're not staying, Drusilla?"

"Oh, Drusilla has another appointment," Asterisk explained. "We were just playing catch-up as she's been away. It actually wasn't Thursday I wanted to talk to you about. It was something else."

Collegial farewells were exchanged. Asterisk waved gallantly at Drusilla as she departed.

"I wanted to talk with you about a formal complaint in my possession," Asterisk began once the door had been closed. "It's about PVC McNamara and it's from Elfyn Dethbridge."

Redman guffawed and rolled his eyes at the same time. "Is this about what I think it's about? Nigel, you know as well as I do that you can stamp on this. The PVCs have a virtual forcefield around them, Short of embezzlement, or gross negligence, or doing the kinds of things Sir Evan Covet did, grievances about senior managers are never allowed to become formal. They get strangled, or otherwise silenced, at birth. And I bet this one isn't even alive to begin with. And he's your deputy. You can surely silence him."

"That was the case in the previous dispensation, yes, but this VC is keen to have things like this handled more by the book."

"Can I see it?"

"Unfortunately no, because it's confidential, of course. By the very book it must be, you see. Besides, I'm not technically involved. Formal complaints must be directed to the manager of the person accused, which in this case is the VC. Elfyn was naturally a little nervous about the form of words he should use to the VC and thus he discussed it with me and showed me his draft. I did all I could to discourage him, but on this matter he is displaying an unusual amount of nerve. I am seeing him later this morning. He is quite determined to force the issue. He's like a little volcano, to be honest. It's as if he's blown his top after years of grumbling."

"He has always detested Robert. They've never got on. But this is all over nothing. There's no case."

"Well, I don't know," Asterisk dissented. "He claims Robert called him *a fucking gaylord* in a public place on the employer's premises during normal working hours. And what with the recent silent LGBT revolution, that has perforce to be treated with all the same seeming seriousness as calling a black man a nigger to his face. These debacles can turn into employment tribunals if you're not careful. And he says he has a witness: *you*."

"Me?" Redman scoffed. "I don't think so. It was out there in the quadrangle, on the morning of the arrests. Robert did refer to someone using those words. But it wasn't Elfyn. He didn't even know Elfyn was there. He had his back to him and he was talking to me. But I told Elfyn all this already."

"How do you mean?"

"I told him on the spot, at the very moment, as well as later that morning, over in the School of English, when he buttonholed me about it in a little hissy fit."

"He hasn't said anything about talking it over with you, not in the statement of grievance or in our conversations."

Redman digested this information uncomfortably. "Ah, I see."

"Do you think he's relying on the VC's likely, er, sympathies about, er, offence of this kind?"

"It's more cunning," said Redman. "Robert was referring *to the VC* and Elfyn knows it. We had both just met him for the first time. I didn't explicitly tell Elfyn that the VC was the *fucking gaylord* alluded to but he had worked it out. What he wants to do is call me as a witness to a grievance committee chaired by the VC and have it revealed that Robert, who is now in a direct working relationship with Spooner, because he has been gifted Vice Chancellorian preferment, said such a vile thing about him in public hearing just a few weeks ago. The intention isn't for Elfyn's offence to be acknowledged. He wants to engineer circumstances so that the VC and Robert are at personal loggerheads. What a nasty little plan!"

Asterisk pondered for a moment. "It's not in anyone's interests for this to happen."

"No," agreed Redman. "But I can think of a simple

solution."

Asterisk's brows rose. "Which is?"

"I could lie. I could simply deny that Robert said any such thing."

Asterisk cleared his throat. "I foresee a problem. I mean, need I say, there is obviously an ethical problem, and so to solve that let's both agree right now that this conversation we're having never happened. But I really mean there is the practical problem of PVC McNamara agreeing to lie also. And I must say, I've become uneasy about lies when they are made a matter of record. They're more readily discoverable when they are in writing."

"It won't get that far. Neither me nor Robert will have to lie."

"How come?"

"Because you will indeed tell Elfyn that we had this conversation. And you will tell him that I denied that Robert said any such thing. He must have been misheard. It's an echoey box, the quadrangle. Elfyn won't even file the grievance if he knows I won't play ball. His entire case rests on my confirmation or Robert's admission. He is probably expecting Robert to deny it. But if he thinks I will also deny it, he'll know his case will be empty."

"So," said Asterisk, "you won't have to lie, if I am prepared to lie? I mean, you did not deny it. You did confirm it."

"I did," said Redman. "But *that part* of the discussion, let's agree, did not happen. The conversation which did happen was the one I just imagined. Or do you have moral reservations about lying to Elfyn to ruin this pathetic stratagem of his?"

Asterisk's expression brightened. "Oh no," he answered. "Not at all."

*

When Redman left Asterisk some minutes later, he was surprised to see Drusilla loitering at the end of the corridor with McNamara, giggling like a girl while he boomed out hearty laughter like Santa Claus, his hand on his stomach. He reflected that McNamara's jolliness quotient was spiking. There had been the half smile just fifteen minutes before. Now, as he walked with him towards the elevator, Drusilla having once more made her excuses to Redman and taken her leave, he saw from the corner of his eye that the older man was broadly beaming, standing more erectly, and altogether cutting a figure of recently enhanced gravity.

"So Spooner agreed, about Poon?" Redman asked.

"Yes," smiled McNamara. "He was over the moon about everything. He didn't even advert to the Trump dimension. I did. I expressed some regret at having not elaborated on my single-word affirmation re The Donald. But Spooner dismissed this as a bagatelle. What he did say was that he thought I should now be on the platform when Trump speaks on Thursday. He wants me to meet him."

"Oh, hell."

They stepped into the elevator and began their whirring ascent.

"It's not a problem," replied McNamara with some levity. "It should be entertaining. Also, don't forget, the Trump money is going to my Faculty and to the Faculty for which I bear staffing responsibility. So it's quite fitting."

Redman pulled a face. "The Faculty *for which I bear staffing responsibility*? Listen to yourself. You're talking like a senior management memo already. Atlas with the world on his shoulders."

McNamara laughed self-deprecatingly as they debouched. Again, Redman thought, behold the waves of amused light-heartedness emanating most untypically from the man. "I apologise. And what did Asterisk have to say?"

"Nothing to report," Redman lied.

They had arrived at their destination: room D4(b). McNamara rapped vigorously on the door. He did not wait for an invitation to enter, and stepped into the room ahead of Redman.

Avril Poon looked up from behind her desk. She remained seated. "PVC McNamara!" she hailed him. "But you're wearing fine silk, not PVC at all! I don't believe we have an appointment. And, wow, Vice Dean Redman too! And you are wearing a suit as well! What smart gentlemen you both are!"

"I regret the unheralded intrusion, Avril," McNamara said. "It's a somewhat urgent matter, and should not take very long. May we sit?"

All of them gathered around the teaching table in the middle of the room.

"We are hoping that you can assist us in a matter of security," commenced McNamara, "and the reason it is we who are speaking to you rather than the Vice Chancellor or the Registrar is that it concerns the activities of the Union. In short, we would be grateful to know what the intentions of the Union are with regard to its involvement in the demonstration planned for Thursday, and to offer some guidance from the University which we trust you will observe."

An ironic smile was twitching at the corners of Poon's mouth long before this mini-speech had concluded. At its end she shook her head ruefully but gently. "You two," she said witheringly. "You come in here like the Kray twins, but why should I be surprised? After all, I know

181

you are both arrant liars. It was in this very room, not four months ago, PVC McNamara, that you took a hidden microphone from behind that picture of Patrick Stewart over there, and showed me another two microphones, and then both of you implied that I was a lunatic by ever-after denying the existence of those bugs, planted by a Vice Chancellor to spy on the elected representatives of his staff. Forgive me, but I don't trust liars. You have no right to any information about the Union's activities. Neither of you is even a UCU member."

McNamara, now glowering, took a breath. "That's not all we covered up, Avril. You want to talk about Odiumgate? You really want to talk about what was concealed that could still do damage to the living rather than just the dead? You remember Jane Blake? I never did tell you, did I, that she told me all about you and her? Or that we have a document in her hand that confirms, with details, claims about the sexual advances you made on her?"

Redman was sure he saw Poon blush, despite the Indian darkness of her face. He chipped in. "You see, we think the lid should be kept on private stuff like that unless there is some overwhelming benefit in exposing it."

"If, for example," added McNamara, "the Union were to withdraw from its involvement in the demonstration on Thursday, that would be an irresistible argument for ensuring that your predation towards Jane Blake remained discreetly concealed."

Poon looked acidly from one to the other. Seconds passed before she replied. "So, bullies, blackmailers, as well as liars, is what you are. Look at you. It's like *Animal Farm* without the revolution: you two pigs haven't overthrown Farmer Jones, you've simply moved out of your sty into the farmhouse with him and are walking around on two legs, or rather in two suits. You, Napoleon, you have the gall to use the word *predation*. You have just thrown into doubt the employment of hundreds of staff in China in the blink of an eye, given them summary notice and abandoned them to the *depredations* of the Chinese government. Just like that! You gave no thought to the consequences for them, did you? I thought not. And now, in the kind of backstairs manoeuvre that so typifies people of your nature, you both emerge from the disguises you have worn all your lives."

"People of our nature?" exclaimed Redman. "Said the Brahmin."

"Oh, cut it, Snowball. By the way, which public school did you go to? You think I didn't know? I saw you once in the coffee bar, reading Wodehouse and laughing. Dead giveaway. The answer to your request is an unnegotiable no. I'm no angel, but I'm not going to have my arm twisted because you have some embarrassing private details about me that you could spill to the world. Do what you like. Now fuck off out of my office, you cock-in-an-asshole combo."

It hadn't gone well, Redman reflected as he and McNamara retreated to the elevator.

"Did I hear her right?" McNamara said.

"Yes."

"She called us a cock-in-an-asshole combo."

"I don't think there was any actual suggestion that we are co-members of her gay entourage. I think she was just being super-rude."

"I was wondering which of us was the cock and which the asshole."

"My money is on me being the asshole. Shall we make

a formal complaint?"

McNamara grinned at the playfully proposed idea. Still happy, Redman noted.

They parted. McNamara had a Management Board meeting to attend. Redman dawdled over to his office in the School of English. Despite the *contretemps* with Poon, he was beginning to feel some of the thrills of intrigue, the tiny shots of adrenalin that seemed to be a reward for scheming, bluffing, and threatening, even when, as on this occasion, they failed to secure their end. The failure merely made one's mind race in order to devise a more successful means of entrapping the enemy.

He picked up the phone and called Lorraine at home.

"I was thinking I might leave early and come straight to yours," he said. "I could be there in half an hour."

"There's early and there's *early*," Lorraine replied. "Forgive me, as someone with fixed hours of work, for thinking that ten on a Monday morning is mighty soon to be knocking off work. In any case, I'm going out for a few hours."

"Later, then. I was thinking we could do something a bit different."

"Different from what?"

"Different from usual. I mean, I could come straight in the door, we could agree that there would be no talk, I could push you up against the wall, right there in your hallway."

"I see."

"I could pull up your skirt and give it to you, standing up –"

"I'm not wearing a skirt," protested Lorraine. "I'm wearing an old pair of jeans."

"You could change."

"I don't want to change."

Undeterred by her lack of cooperation, Redman continued suavely. "Alright, then, jeans it is. I shall just have to throw you on the bed and peel them off."

"Have to?" repeated Lorraine. "No, you don't *have to*."

"I mean, I'd like to."

"Clearly."

"I could give it to you all afternoon."

"You could."

"You know, not so much romance as a good hard dirty fucking."

"I get the picture."

"Is that a yes?"

There was a brief but heavy silence.

"What do you think, James?"

The lack of affirmation finally stopped Redman in his tracks. "It doesn't sound like a yes," he acknowledged.

"No," said Lorraine, "it's not. Stay at work, James. Don't come to mine at all today. I will speak to you again when your need for a whore has passed."

The line went dead.

It hadn't, Redman reflected, gone well.

"Now, ladies and gentlemen," Spooner was saying in the splendour of his office to his seven Pro-Vice Chancellors and his Registrar, "now that we have welcomed Professor McNamara to his first Management Board meeting, and heard his summary report on China, it's time for my update on the visit of President Trump this coming Thursday. You can expect, from tomorrow, a great deal of Secret Service activity in this building and the routes to it, because the cheque-handover ceremony will take place in the Great Hall. Be aware that Secret Service agents are permitted to, and do, carry firearms, though they will not be armed when they interview every individual, including yourselves, who is likely to come into contact or close proximity to the President. They will brief you on decorum and other matters of conduct. Please follow their advice. Your individual appointments with the Secret Service are scheduled for tomorrow and you can find the times and venue in the briefing pack before you. Please ensure that you read everything in there before Thursday.

"I should say that, if Whitehall was already hopping mad with us – or more specifically, with me – over China, it's absolutely incandescent about the Trump visit. I can confirm with some pleasure that the Prime Minister, though she was, I know, sorely tempted, will not be paying us a visit in order to be the most prominent person to shake the President's hand on his first visit to the country since his electoral victory. Nothing has been or will be said in public, but I got a personal roasting from another woman in Number 10 on the phone over the weekend. That's how I know she's not coming. President Trump is diffident about meeting her now in any case: he told me he wasn't very impressed with her when she came to the White House the other month, and he prefers to wait for the full pomp and ceremony of a state visit, when she'll be eclipsed in the American press by his meeting the Queen. Her absence makes the security issues a little less vexing.

"We do, however, still have the problem of the planned demonstration to contend with. We have had meetings with the police, and the police have had meetings with those responsible for organising the protest. But we do not know exactly what shape the event is likely to take. The advice we initially received was that we should shut out anyone not officially involved from all three access routes entered from the north, east and west entrances to the campus. We can do this, as inside the gates, legally speaking, they are all private roads. In effect, this would have meant that the protest could take place only outside the campus perimeter, very far from this building. However, the projected numbers expected to attend occupy a range from the enormous to the colossal, something between fifty and one hundred thousand people. If all of them are kept outside the perimeter, they will choke every arterial road around us and the entire city will soon be gridlocked for hours. There are concerns about the effects on residents in properties nearby. We have therefore taken the decision to turn this building, and this building alone, into Fort Knox. The President will arrive in a chopper and land right out there in the quadrangle of what he calls 'my own British Trump Tower'. The ceremony is expected to last merely minutes. The invited guests in the Great Hall, as well as the media, using biometric security passes issued for the occasion, will have to check in an hour before its commencement. When it's over, he will be helicoptered off again, and we shall be forty million pounds richer, with more on the way. Pray, please, for yet a further fall in the international value of sterling between now and Thursday. I worked out last night that every cent the pound goes down is worth about ten new academic posts to us.

"We intend to be cooperative with the demonstrators, as long as they stay outside this bunker, of course. We do intend to advertise the fact of those Secret Service guns as a deterrent to any idea of their trying to gain entry to this building. We have plenty of open spaces on campus and they will generally be as free as any member of the public is to enter and ramble. There will be massive security on all buildings, of course, particularly science buildings. We are pulling out all the stops on the catering front, and jacking up the prices. Indeed, the feeding of the fifty-plus thousand is expected to net us something between a quarter and half a million on a single day. That might just cover the cost of the extra security. There will, moreover, be large stages erected about fifty metres from this building, on which the protesters, or their spokespersons, will be at liberty to orate. This should give the lie to the idea that we frown on freedom of speech. We are, quite literally, providing them with the platform on which to speak. In reality, the two stages will act as an outer shield for us, as the crowds shall be corralled on the far side of them. Are there any questions?"

McNamara surveyed the array of professorial heads around the table, then ended the short hiatus.

"Not so much a question," he said, "as a probe, a seeking-out of views. It concerns the press. I've already been approached, directly, for comment on the Trump visit. Perhaps others have or will be too."

"Ah," Spooner piped up. "Yes, thank you. No need for a seeking-out of views, in fact. Only two people henceforth will talk to the media, myself and our Communications Officer, Drusilla Frost. If you are contacted by any reporters, refer them in the first instance to Drusilla. Say nothing, offer no comment or opinion, keep shtum."

He looked at McNamara. McNamara nodded. "I concur," he concurred. "I think it's easier for each of us that way, as well as promising to guarantee consistency in the University's reported pronouncements."

"No, you listen to me, Elfyn," Redman heard himself growling down his office phone in an unusually menacing voice. "There's not that much difference between a lie and a deliberate failure to tell the whole truth. And that's what you're doing. Take it from me, I've seen people not that dissimilar to you try to play similar doggy tricks in front of a Vice Chancellor. It didn't turn out well for them. They didn't think it through." He allowed his throat to relax, and the force in his voice eased. "Say you brought your complaint before a grievance committee, and called me as a witness, and I came in and agreed, yes, Professor McNamara did say those words, but he was most definitely not referring to Mr Dethbridge, and I told Mr Dethbridge so, twice. In your wish-fulfilment fantasy of what happens after that, you think the next question is going to be, well, to whom *was* he referring? But it isn't. The obvious next question is, is this true, Mr Dethbridge? Did Dr Redman indeed apprise you, not once but twice, of the fact that Professor McNamara was referring to someone else? And if so, if you knew that, why are you wasting our time with this misleading complaint? Do you think we care that Professor McNamara let rip an unguarded, politically incorrect accusation in a private conversation, if no offence was caused to the object of his insult? Do you imagine that we are more concerned about that than about an attempt by an administrator to undermine a senior officer of the University less than a fortnight after he has assumed his post? Aware as you are of recent scandals in the management of the University, Mr Dethbridge, is it your objective to drag the University down further into the mire? And so on. And what if you even got past these shockwaves of negative reaction and managed, somehow, to elicit a statement to the fact that Professor McNamara was actually referring to the Vice Chancellor. What? You are going to out Spooner officially in a grievance committee at which he is present, *which he is personally chairing*, in front of others, and on record?

It will be you, then, won't it, who is drawing attention to the Vice Chancellor's gaylordiness? How can you ever have thought that such a situation could end anything but badly for you?"

He could hear Dethbridge's shallow breathing in the earpiece.

"In a way," Redman added with a small air of munificence, "I'm kind of doing you a favour in stopping you."

The line went dead.

Chapter Twelve

Two days later, Redman found himself stepping, with a kind of resentment and dread, into the University Staff Club. A few years before, an internal survey had come round whose last question had been, "What single change would make you come to the Staff Club more frequently?" He had answered, "Its conversion to a teaching building." Soon afterwards the Club had abandoned its membership fee and structure and anyone in an eligible "job family" (as the current contracts so wholesomely put it) was free to wander in. It made its money by jacking up the food and drink prices and renting out rooms to other parts of the University in need of a cosy central location where catering could readily be laid on. So much in demand were its wood-panelled nooks that an extra such room had been created by throwing out the snooker table. The only times Redman had found himself within ten metres of the Club's cracked brown leather sofas and nineteenth century newspaper rack were when attendance at some or other University meeting required him to be there. He had never gone through its mock-country house portal voluntarily or in response to some sociable invitation.

But now he had come to meet McNamara there.

McNamara had once had a similar distaste for the Club – or was it for the staff? – but since his ascension to the status of equerry, he had rapidly been converted to the idea (and, even worse, the reality) that the Club was the best place on campus for senior managers to do all of the informal cajoling and gladhanding and threatening that was a necessary part of their success in the role. These were activities, everyone seemed silently to agree, that it would be too unseemly to perform in an official, not to say minuted, meeting.

McNamara had let it be known to Redman that he had been spending a lot of time in the Club this week. With the Trump money about to create the most magnificent sunrise the Arts and Humanities and Social Science Faculties had ever witnessed, lots of Heads of School, especially in the Arts Faculty for which he now had control of staffing, wanted McNamara to know how much they had enjoyed his last book, that they remembered the name of his ex-wife and two sons, and, incidental to the personally flattering courtliness which governed most of their speech, that he would be very impressed to visit their Departments to see the "world class" academic initiatives suddenly taking root in every single one of them.

Redman half-expected that McNamara might by now be pulsing with the slight glow of a provincial Brando. He found him in the bar, smiling, as was his wont these days, with the particular kind of geniality that comes only after a substantial period spent exercising patronage. A fat black diary – a first for McNamara, that – lay on the table before him, a Mont Blanc Meisterstück LeGrand pen inserted between its pages. His attire was as sable as the pen's resin, but he was matt to its scintillating surface. Redman judged that he had none of the anticipated charisma that might parallel its gold-coated details or the white star emblem which surmounted it. He looked tired without, unpolished. Drinking beside him was not a Head of School but Stoner, in blinding all-white, looking as ever like man who could command a fee in a detergent commercial.

"Christ, it's ebony and ivory," said Redman, reaching out to shake Stoner's hand. "Last time I heard from you, you had just visited Yunus at his country retreat."

McNamara looked at Stoner. "I didn't know that," he said. "Isn't that like, what, Graham Greene visiting Kim Philby?"

Stoner put his filled pipe in his mouth, recalled that he was not allowed to smoke it indoors, sighed, and let it fall to his knee. He looked as if he were about to say what he indeed considered saying, which was no more contestatory than, "I have adopted a rule to be neither flattered or ruffled by personal comparisons." But as he conned these words over hypercritically – which he did very rapidly, because Stoner was a kind of computer which by default processed diplomatic outputs and only infrequently went haywire – he considered that they might suggest he was too much the Asimovian law-bound robot. What he said instead was, "Did Graham Greene visit Kim Philby? I didn't know *that*."

"He means in Moscow, after Philby defected," Redman chipped in. "Of course, he knew Philby before. Philby was his boss at MI6."

"Was Graham Greene in MI6?" said Stoner. "I didn't know that either. I assure you I have nothing to do with MI6."

"Come to think of it," McNamara went on, pursuing the tangent, "I can't get my head around Greene's favourability towards the USSR. I mean, it was long after

Hungary. Everyone else was running away from the Soviet Communist Party. He went sprinting towards it with open arms."

"Maybe he just wanted to visit an old mate," said Stoner. "You know, damn what anyone thinks, the man's a close personal friend, that kind of thing. Personal loyalty that refuses to be contaminated by societal condemnation. Quite a good impulse. An indissoluble bond based on human fellow feeling."

"No," said McNamara dismissively. "He was all over Eastern Europe through two decades, hardly just Russia, hardly just once, and hardly just to meet Philby."

"He thought Catholicism and Communism were reconcilable," Redman explained.

"He did?" said Stoner quizzically. "Well, they're not. Any fool could have told him that. Stupid man."

"But," said McNamara, "it was more complicated than that. He knew that meeting Philby in particular would cause a furore in the press and upset the Establishment apple cart. They were also probably worried what Philby might tell him which he might later reveal. No such things would motivate you to visit Yunus, of course, William. You are more the simple personal loyalty type, right?"

Stoner acknowledged that his attempt to deflect the conversation had been defeated. "You want to know about the meeting with Yunus? Fair enough. It was depressing. You should understand that I have in my mind an intellectually orientated, articulate, sophisticated young man I have come to know, I thought well, over a decent interval. I consider him rational and reasonable. I am not really too attentive to his political side. That showed itself only occasionally in any case. I had him down as passionate, perhaps a little idealistic and romantic about such matters, as people of his age tend to be, but not in any way extreme or rigidly programmatic. Mostly we talked about books and north Africa and, of course, the wonderful thing was that we spoke in Arabic. His Arabic is beautiful, by the way. In fact, the ironic thing is, I don't think he could say in Arabic the things he said to me in English. His inauthenticity would have rung hollow in his mother tongue. As this suggests, the person I met at the meeting seemed an entirely different creature. Would I say we quarreled? No. But I told him what I thought about his opportunism, the lack of any foundation for his public crusade, the harm he was likely doing himself. He was subdued, but his eyes were quickly flashing betrayal. A little bit dramatic. I sometimes thought I heard a stirring soundtrack filling the silences. He told me nothing that would be of any use to you two, though, if that's why you're interested. If he had, I'd let you in on it. Now I must step outside for a smoke. Excuse me, chaps."

As Stoner had left, McNamara went to the bar and ordered Redman a drink.

"You already have a tab?" said Redman.

McNamara rolled his eyes. "Thank you for coming. I've had so little time, and I have to go to a dinner this evening. How is Lorraine?"

"I don't know," said Redman wearily, sipping at his pint. "I haven't seen her since Sunday, three days now. I have spoken to her on the phone, of course, but she seems to be in a very discontented state of mind. I'm not sure if her discontent is with me as well as this place. She certainly wants me to stay away. But on the other score she appears to have arrived at the conclusion that universities constitute one of the circles of hell. She's been applying for jobs elsewhere, even in secondary schools, would you believe. Maybe she's right. Maybe it would be better if we didn't work in the same corridor."

McNamara looked sympathetic. "Well, of course, the death threats, the awful media coverage, the slapdash way we overlooked her distress, these will all have affected her deeply."

Redman looked confused. "We?" he said.

"University management," McNamara explained.

"Oh. That's who *we* is now. I see. Not you and me."

McNamara gave a short laugh. "I apologise. I have been talking in this corporate academic officialese all day."

"If you're accepting collective responsibility, you could always persuade them to do something to help her," Redman suggested.

McNamara's head tilted to one side. "That's more something you'd have to take to the Registrar, given that she's an administrator."

"I've already pulled one favour with him recently," Redman said. "I don't think I can push my luck."

McNamara nodded, "I'm sorry. I've been trying to observe the rather delicate separation of powers around here. I'd rather promised myself not to meddle in domains which are not my own."

Redman shrugged. "Okay. But you didn't ask me here to talk about Lorraine."

"No," McNamara acknowledged. "I was hoping to sound you out about tomorrow."

"What about it? I know nothing more about what's planned. People seem much more suspicious of me now that I am Vice Dean. The usually loud rumour mill has stopped grinding in my vicinity. The gossip waterfall which seemed to follow me and rain on me continuously for years has dried up overnight."

"I know the feeling," McNamara agreed. "Actually, it was something specific I was going to ask you. As you know, I will be immured in the Great Hall tomorrow from an hour before Trump arrives. I understand that Spooner will be all wired up with a comms unit in his ear to give him real time updates on Trump's approach. That's mainly a line to the Secret Service. Someone else is doing the same thing with respect to our own security. But no one seems to be keeping a trained gaze on the demonstration itself. You know, what's happening, who's there..."

"What are you asking?"

"I was wondering if you would be my eyes and ears outside the Trump Building. You know, talk to me on the phone, tell me what's going on, maybe film it."

"Film it?"

"Yes."

"Why?"

"Who can tell? Might be evidence if anything goes wrong. Would allow me to identify those in attendance."

"Why do you want to know who's in attendance? I mean, it sounds like you want to mark their cards."

McNamara harrumphed. "Oh, come on, James, let's not be naïve. We both know it's part of winning any struggle that you need to know who's up against you. There will be numerous University security cameras filming the event, so I don't see what's so strange about making a video. But I won't have personal access to the security footage. I need to know, when I encounter these members of staff at a later date, that if they feel strongly enough in their views about the Trump money and the Odium Two, views which they know are diametrically opposed to my own, that they'll go so far as to attend the first political demonstration of any substance in all my years at Odium. Why should I have to second guess their position when they already know mine?"

"*Go so far as to attend*? That's not dreadfully far, is it? I mean, it's hardly the last word in political activism, more the first, no? And the difference between you and them is that you are officially a publicly accountable figure while they are private individuals. You also happen to have a degree of power over them, which makes monitoring their extra-employment activities seem a little menacing."

"Extra-employment activities!" McNamara spluttered. "They will be attending in normal working hours! They'll be being paid – by *us*! – while they attend. What's not public about a political demonstration? And as for being publicly accountable, that's exactly what attending a protest event is: showing that you are prepared to account for your beliefs *in public*. They don't have rights of privacy in public because of the entirely antithetical meanings of the words *private* and *public*."

Redman was shaking his head. "I don't believe you. You, a senior manager, are asking me to spy on the members of staff attending a political event, so that you can personally identify them in a way that, by your own admission, might influence your later treatment of them, or the decisions you take about them, in the workplace. How did we get here? Where exactly did we take the wrong turning? Was it a long time ago or was it just recently? Why do I hear nothing about Buddha from you these days?"

All through Redman's questioning McNamara had been pulling his oh-don't-be-so-bloody-ridiculous face. But now it dropped into a more congenial mask, as all further colloquy between the two was inhibited by the entrance of Nigel Asterisk. He looked nervous. He approached them directly and sat with them.

"I was told you were here," he said to McNamara. "And James, how convenient, because this concerns you too. Tell me, Robert, you must have had your security interview by now, yes?"

"With the Secret Service?" said McNamara.

"Yes," said Asterisk.

McNamara nodded.

"But was there another man there, a different man from the one who interviewed you?"

"There were a couple of other guys."

"I mean a tall, hefty guy, about forty, red hair."

"Yes, there was."

"Did he speak to you?"

"At the end, yes. He showed me a photograph and asked me if I'd ever seen the man in it."

"Did you ask him why?"

"Why he was asking me?"

"Yes."

"No. I said no, I'd never seen the guy."

"I see," said Asterisk. "Let me get a scotch." He was away for a moment at the bar. When he returned to his seat, he said, "I asked why."

McNamara allowed a second to pass. "And what did he answer?"

Asterisk swilled a mouthful of whisky. "Do you think that makes me sound suspicious?"

Redman intervened. "Why would it make you sound suspicious?"

Asterisk leaned in to them, lowering his voice. "It was a photograph of Professor Buckrack," he breathed.

This information caused a prolonged three-way triangular exchange of glances so expressive that *The Good, the Bad and the Ugly* seemed momentarily to have a real-life rival. However, the mood quickly descended into soap opera or, at best, police procedural.

"He didn't explain why," said Asterisk. "He just maintained a long silence and repeated the question. I mean, where's the decency? How come he gets to ask me questions and I have to answer them, but he doesn't have to answer a single question I put to him?"

"Maybe," said Redman, "that was your mistake. You assumed without questioning that he had the power to do so."

"Or," said Asterisk, "I correctly inferred that he had a lot more power than I do."

"So," asked McNamara, "did you tell him no?"

"I told him yes!" exclaimed Asterisk. "I'm not going to lie to the CIA or the FBI or whatever he was."

"They have no jurisdiction," Redman said.

"It all happened rather fast, too fast to think. It seemed to be part of the Security Service interview at first, just another question. So I told the truth. Unlike you, Robert, I know what Professor Cannon Buckrack looks like. I said yes, and I gave his name."

The trio indulged in a further spaghetti-westernish moment.

"You'd have done better to lie," said Redman.

"How could I possibly lie," protested Asterisk, "about one of the Professors on my own staff? For god's sake, he's still on the books. The last phone call I got from Covet said Buckrack would be disappearing off the scene but to let his contract run its course. I didn't pay much attention there and then, not least because Covet had been suspended from office at the time. But later, when I came to reflect on it, I agreed it best to leave our employment of Buckrack in place until the end of this academic year. If he kept getting the salary, he'd be more likely stay away. And none of us wants him back."

Redman and McNamara exchanged glances shiftily. "That we didn't know," said Redman. "But you could have corrected the lie later if it ever bounced back to you, said you hadn't looked at the photo carefully enough."

"There were other people who met Buckrack," said Asterisk, "like those at the Disclosure Committee. They would have identified him anyway when they were interviewed. Whatever, the main reason I am telling you both this is that I need to know you've got my back."

He was not made comfortable by the mystified expressions on the faces of Redman and McNamara. He became more persuasive. "Listen, we're all in this together. Why is anyone asking questions about Buck-rack? How much do they know? What if they know about the bugs? We all participated in their concealment. How is that going to play out for us if it ever becomes open knowledge? A University senior management secretly recording the conversations of elected trades Union officers? And then a deliberate cover-up by three people, fiddling with evidence?"

"I think it will play out rather more badly for you than for us, Nigel," Redman said. "After all, we were two of the people whose rooms were bugged. It was *you* who made the arrangements for Buckrack to steal the evidence. Our reasons for concealing the existence of the bugs were not morally equivalent to yours."

"No, he's right, James," said McNamara. "This is something we must try to keep the lid on. We can't confide in the current VC, he wasn't here then, and he knows nothing, and moreover wants to know nothing. If this got out it would be just another scandal, a revivified corpse of a dead scandal. We've got enough on our plate."

Redman cleared his throat and looked at Asterisk.

"Why would the CIA or the FBI be interested in the internal shenanigans of an English university? It's obvious: it's Buckrack they're interested in. Look for the American."

"There is that," said McNamara. "Mind you, there's more than one American."

"How do you mean?" said Asterisk warily.

"Jane Blake," said McNamara. "She was an American, moreover one murdered, so the verdict read, by a British subject. That would seem to me to be the obvious crime we know about that would legitimise the intervention of the US authorities."

"Of course," said Redman. "And she planted the bugs. And if they are looking into her death then there's the whole issue of her Public Disclosure document, which Buckrack was involved in assessing, her affair with Covet... that's a lot of dirty linen."

"*Did* she plant the bugs?" asked McNamara.

"Didn't she?" said Asterisk, and coughed.

"Neither of us really got to the bottom of it," said McNamara. "It was obvious that she had access to my study and to Poon's office, but we could never figure out how she got into James's."

"Well," said Asterisk, "she *was sleeping* with Covet. He could have conjured up a master key from his back pocket. Job done."

"I see," McNamara nodded. "That's the obvious explanation. I am always forgetful about just how slippery the man was."

"I'm not allowed to be slippery," said Asterisk. "I managed to excuse myself pronto on a made-up pretext, but he wants to talk to me tomorrow morning about Buckrack."

"You didn't say no?" said Redman, and then watched

Asterisk shaking his head. "It would have been better had you said no. I repeat: these people have no jurisdiction."

While Redman was repeating himself Asterisk had been getting up his how-could-I-possibly-say-no face. But now it morphed perforce into a merely melancholy mug, and he simply said, "To be continued." The reason was that all further conspiracy among the three had been inhibited by the re-entrance of William Stoner.

Chapter Thirteen

McNamara was awoken on Trump Thursday by what sounded like a military convoy passing through the west entrance of campus, near his Warden's house. Heavy vehicles, their engines growling in low gear, clunked over grates, bounced across sleeping policemen, their hydraulics hissing, occasional electronic bleeps sounding off as one or other of them made some necessary reversing manoeuvre. His attempts to go back to sleep failed. He lay for a while, looking with some satisfaction at the rumpled sheets in the half of the bed Drusilla had vacated last night: she had gone home in order to prepare for her busy day ahead.

At last he got up, and, looking at the clock, decided to do something he had often done, but not for some time. He made a pot of tea and four slices of buttered toast. He put them on a tray with two cups and a small jug of milk and a little bowl of sugar, left the house still in his pyjamas, dressing gown and slippers, and walked slowly towards the gatehouse that stood in the centre of the entrance road. Arriving there, he found the area to be in a great deal more of a hubbub than was customary at this time on a normal weekday morning. As well as the merely one security guard sitting sentry in the gatehouse, a further dozen were strung out along the pavements on the far side of the gate, between the two sets of iron railings on either side. They were guiding and gesticulating at the drivers of vans, cars, buses, mobile homes and motorcycles that formed a long chain tailing back well onto the perimeter road outside the campus. The larger vehicles were being turned into a subsidiary gate that opened into an enormous area of grassy land on the other side of the road from McNamara's house. The land had escaped University buildings expansion by being a little too marshy for architectural construction. Traditionally, it was used, as it was being used now, as a massive car park on University open days or for conference guests. When otherwise vacant, students could sometimes be found playing impromptu games of football or cricket on it. It was already a quarter full.

He crossed to the small upright gatehouse that sat between the electrified exit and entrance barriers. The sentry saw him coming and slid open the cubicle's window.

"Hello, Mr McNamara!"

"I'm sorry, Bill," McNamara said as he stepped onto the small kerb by the gatehouse and passed the tray inside. "This used to be a weekly fixture, but I've been remiss. I can't remember how long it is since we've done it."

"That's alright, Mr McNamara," said the grey-haired Bill, now pouring. "From what I hear, you've been busy."

"That's true." McNamara laughed and took the cup of tea Bill offered.

"We can breakfast at our ease today," said Bill,

nodding towards the other security guards. "They're taking care of most of it so far, filtering it off before it gets to me."

McNamara looked all around. "Did you expect it so early?" he said. "Trump doesn't get here 'til four."

"Oh, it's been all hands on deck since six this morning," Bill replied.

"But this area they're filtering the vehicles into, behind Hooters Hall, won't it get full?"

"For sure," said Bill. "We expect it to be at capacity by ten."

"And they're – am I seeing this right without my glasses? – some of them seem to be pitching tents. Why?"

"Looks like they're intending to stay."

"This was the danger in opening the campus up, that it would become more than a demonstration: an occupation."

"I called it in when we first saw them making camp. But the word back was to let them do what they like as long as it's peaceful. I suppose we'll have to deal with any squatters tomorrow. The vital thing seems to be to keep them a certain distance from the Trump Building but otherwise allow them free rein. One of us went over and talked to a few of the campers, but they said the tents were just covering in case of rain. They weren't too polite."

Much of this was said through mouthfuls of heartily consumed toast. McNamara became aware of two familiar blurred figures becoming larger on the right pavement. It was Redman, in shorts and a singlet, running in to work with his dog, both of them slaloming between the chain of security guards.

"Welcome to Haight Ashbury!" Redman greeted them as he came into focus.

McNamara said his goodbyes to Bill and promised to return for the tray. He had learned what he wanted to know: something larger than a one-off protest seemed to have been planned.

"Would you like to come inside?" McNamara said to Redman, looking with some ironic distaste at the dog. "I'm sure I could find him a soft toy to rape."

Redman acquiesced. On the short walk to McNamara's house, he said, "I thought more about your request. I'll watch and report on the demonstration outside the Trump Building, but I won't video it. I'll note the presence of anyone we mutually detest. How's that?"

"That's good enough," said McNamara. "Thank you."

Once inside, he made coffee and reported on his conversation with Bill.

"I've also been thinking a lot," he began when they were seated, "about the discussion we had last night after William returned and Asterisk left. I find his idea of the university to be intellectually indefensible these days, indeed on any day for the last hundred years, at least in Britain, but I think also anywhere else. He's almost Kantian, is William, what with the belief he has in the power of the university, properly managed, to deliver truth by means of reason. It's nearly a comic-book notion now, the kind of thing believed by people who have never been to university, or have had only a passing acquaintance with one. They think it's full of pulsating superior brains and boffins and is run on a model of the contemplative life, some kind of philosophical hothouse shot through with the rays of enlightened humanism."

"Whereas you and I know it," said Redman, "as an institution for the reproduction and maintenance of the technician class of the nation state. Or at least, that's how we knew it as students, with free tuition and maintenance grants for the small minority permitted entry. It stopped being that while I was a postgrad student, though I didn't notice that so much until I started teaching here. It got postmodernised some time in the early nineties."

"It started to get postmodernised, more precisely, in 1992, because of the Maastricht Treaty and its creation of the EU," McNamara explained. "The need for integration with other EU education systems led to the creation of interchangeable units of assessment and credit, so that students could move freely, on transfer or exchange, between European universities. This was shortly before your time. From that moment on students were no longer our great future natural resource in need of careful harnessing. They became little more than a market to be selling to, and all caps were instantly taken off international recruitment. We did well because, frankly, most continental European universities are so crap that even Odium looks decent beside them. Students were no longer viewed as a restricted reservoir of talent to be trained up at the state's cost to occupy pre-designated roles in the national economy, as we could just as well have a German doing a job in Britain as a Brit. The change was pretty instant as far as the economic dimension went, but it takes far longer for such a change to be accepted or even processed ideologically."

"We never accepted it," Redman agreed. "It's not that we were particularly enamoured of being at the service of the state, but it assured us of an institutional existence that wasn't based on commerce, and consequently we discharged a well-defined public function. When the state washed its hands of economic responsibility for us, and turned us loose, we became little different from national or multinational companies, except that we were not permitted to have shareholders or turn a profit. Instead, what we had to turn were the equivalent of circus tricks in order to get customers, the most spectacular of which were our forays into China and India."

"Which," said McNamara, "are now at an end. Or at least China, the bigger of the two enterprises, is. And now, with Brexit, the EU is also soon to be at an end, at least for us. So we would appear to be at another turning point."

"A reversal?" Redman thought aloud. "You think we are going to spend the next twenty-five years getting back to where we were in 1991? That seems doubtful."

"I agree," said McNamara. "I don't see us returning to anything as civic-minded either. So much else has changed. Of course it is tempting to explain the whole thing as the idea of a university simply being subjected to zigzags and U-turns according to whatever way the trade winds of contemporary capitalism are blowing. There are some signs that a reversal of sorts will happen in parts of the economy where there is a deficiency of supply. Apparently foreign doctors are already in decline in the NHS even though we are at least two years out from the Brexit axe falling. They are abandoning the ship long before she sinks, not least because the British pound is now worth close to jack shit. I was told the other day that the government is already stumping up money for increased quotas in next year's intake in the Nursing and Medical schools, despite all economic plans for the next eighteen months having been already irrevocably signed and triple sealed. But in our neck of the woods that will hardly matter. Englishness or Britishness was the bottle our genie escaped from, so I see no mass return to Eng. Lit., your subject, as the precious purveyor of national identity it was once imagined to be. Nor do I see any likelihood that my School will go back to teaching Politics on the assumption that half our graduates will be doing British civil service exams at the end of it. Not a lot is clear. We may be wrong to overestimate the power of the current anti-globalisation wave. The era of the dominance of transnational capital won't end simply because the British and American governments seek greater isolation. This might just be a blip."

"Nonetheless," guessed Redman, "you feel in your gut that the Trump-Odium marriage signifies something new, a departure? It's a wave to be followed by other similar waves?"

"I do," said McNamara. "But we're going to be so pre-occupied just keeping our heads above water that we won't be able to pay much attention to what the weather is like around us. We're swimming blind."

"*You're* swimming blind," Redman corrected him. "You have a say in what's going to happen. Me, I'm not swimming at all. I'm well under the surface, thrashing about."

Civic. It was a word, Redman pondered as he left McNamara's house, dog in tow on a lead, that had gone the way of *public service* and *collegiate*. Quaint terms now. They belonged to an irrecoverable age in which noble institutions were defined by being outside the usual nexus of commercial exchange and described using honourable, untainted words. The University certainly maintained a topographical and architectural facade which *civic* described well, having been erected on an old country estate, the Trump Building assuming a variety of roles as needed, now a kind of manor house, now a town hall, now a church, albeit with a mere clock tower rather than a steeple, but, aptly, with an enormous organ in its Great Hall. The entire campus, brooding with seeming benevolence over the town on the highest hill for miles around, appeared detached and above any imaginable fray, though this was a merely phenomenal deception. It was in reality now more like the wartime abbey of Monte Cassino, having long given up the purpose for which its founders had created it, squatted in and contested by rival factions, none of which seemed able or prepared to restore it to its proper function, but all of whom seemed very interested in it for other, more power-driven purposes. No one, least of all he or McNamara, was likely to come with a scourge to drive out the moneymen, overturn their tables, and declare to the hawk-eyed sellers of doves, *take these things hence; make not my Father's house an house of merchandise*. Not in a month of Sundays.

But hardly anything, now, at even this hour of nine on Trump Thursday morning, could be seen of the campus's civic remnants, its splendour of cultivated lawn and well-cut masonry. What met the eyes and assaulted the ears seemed more indicative of a caravanserai. Trailers and vans and pickups and cars and bikes barricaded both sides of the tarmac snaking inwards from the west entrance, the majority of them having mounted the pavements on either side, so that other vehicles could still pass on the road, while pedestrians, hundreds of them, *thousands* of them, squeezed and shuffled among the tight spaces remaining along the very edges. Normally open vistas were blocked by high-sided metal transports of all kinds. There was booming noise, not just of massed chattering voices, but also, inevitably, of blaring music and distorted loudhailers, all of which seemed to make the air crackle and buzz like a that of a fairground. Every twenty metres or so the nose was teased by some new strong savoury smell, now hot dogs, now burgers and onions, now chips. All that was missing was the aroma of candy floss and toffee apples, no doubt absent because there were few children around. There was occasionally, however, even this early, the unmistakable scent of ganja.

The University of Odium may, these days, have had its fate inextricably associated with that of the global market, but one thing was immediately evident: the markets it gambled in did not typically contain the kinds of human specimen cavorting here today. One look at the crowds brought to Redman's mind the now little-heard descriptor *the great unwashed*. Truly, you could indeed tell who lived on the campus and who didn't from tide marks on necks and filth stains behind ears, the general grubbiness of many clothes and the greasiness of many heads of hair. He felt a little like George Orwell in Lancashire. It was no doubt probable that lots of these grey-fleshed creatures were students also, but if so they obviously came from establishments approved (or merely found affordable) by not-well-heeled parents. Redman had not particularly noticed how clean and attractive Odium students were until he was faced with these alternatives. If Odium was a freshwater ornamental pond replete with cichlids and pufferfish, this other lot were so much haddock and cod hoiked directly out of the cold, briny Irish Sea. By their numbers, their natures, and their noisomeness they made the whole campus appear irredeemably ugly, all the while comporting themselves with such casual entitlement that they gave the impression that they owned the place. This was, Redman concluded, because they were not here to study, or do anything otherwise cognitively challenging, but merely to piss about for a day playing politics.

He decided to walk the long way round to the Trump Building, encircling the campus in a loop that would take in most of it. He discovered that it seemed to be sectorised, by accident rather than design. Put bluntly, only about half of it seemed inspired by Roma caravan culture, with its anthem of the diesel generator and signature whiffs of frying meat. Some few hundred metres on, a vast tract of ground on either side of a long curve of road seemed dominated by spontaneous scratch team games, possibly because it was near the sports centre, where the land was flattened and superbly grassed. For reasons which he could not fathom, national flags had been hung out of bedroom windows in halls of residence, as if the day were an international competitive gathering in which patriotism had some role. But he saw no stars and stripes. Lines of protesters shuffled constantly in and out of these residential buildings, whose dining rooms were the mess halls for the day to their army of temporary occupation.

An incline gradually rose in this part of the campus, but it was not before one was atop it that one lost the feeling of being behind the front lines and entered what felt like the political sector. Again, this bore the outward stamp of spectatorial leisure, thousands stamping their feet and rubbing their hands in the chill morning in areas defined by huge batteries of flat-screen televisions, hooked up to each other in arrays which collectively bodied forth images easily ten metres wide by five high. They were all at the moment showing pictures of the empty main stage near the Trump Building, whose barricaded environs had been thronged early on and to which proximity for most was now impossible. Only the really early birds would be able to get within two hundred metres of Trump, who nonetheless would be entirely invisible to all of them, other than what might be seen of him on such screens.

Because Redman worked in the Trump Building, he had been issued with a special pass permitting him limited entry. The instructions that came with it told him to report to a desk in the main library, whence he was taken by a member of staff to a distant door which had to be manually unlocked, then there was another, nearer door, which he was ushered through on his own, and which was duly closed behind him. He found himself in a short corridor, in which four security guards, two men and two women, stood around a full-body backscatter scanner machine that looked as if it had been borrowed from an airport for the day. Once he had submitted to the scan, he was told to descend a set of nearby steps all the way to the bottom. He soon twigged that these steps must give access to the library's underground store of books, but was surprised after several floors to be confronted by a well-lit corridor, guarded at its entry by a further ten security officers, who smilingly permitted him unhindered passage along it. It headed due south, and he soon gathered that this was the beaver's entrance to the Trump Building. Nor was it new. Painting flaked on the walls and some of the strip lighting started to flicker halfway along. There was a right-bearing dog leg at the end, where he encountered yet another security post. A door was opened and closed behind him. He recognised the door on the other side. It was next to an elevator in the basement on the north-facing edge of the building. He had seen it several times before. He had assumed it was a broom cupboard.

He walked upstairs. Mostly the building was deserted, and when it filled up later in the day the permitted hordes of press and media would be in its southernmost wing opposite, where the Great Hall was situated. The School of English was entirely desolate. But Redman had decided to make a regular working day of it for as long as he could, and so entered his office, sat down, turned on his computer, and tried to ignore the perceptible hiss and hum of the massed protestors outside, audible still across distance, over barriers and through closed windows.

Within ten minutes, he received an email from Lorraine. It read, "I thought I'd better tell you that I have an interview for a job at the University of Surleighwick next Tuesday. As you know, my parents live in Yorkshire. I will talk with you further after that." He digested this communication for a few seconds, decided he was not going to reply to it, and found himself assuredly comforted by a response that seemed to well up from somewhere deep within him and made everything seem so much more immediately bearable: *fuck Lorraine.*

Chapter Fourteen

Had anyone been present, several hours later, to see McNamara emerge into the Trump Building from the subterranean tunnel, they would have witnessed the expression of a man who had realised that something seemed very wrong with current circumstances, but who was not sure exactly what.

In other words he was suddenly on edge, on guard. In fact, he had entered the tunnel in a much different, more routine mood. It is hard to imagine, he had consciously thought, that anyone with a reasonable level of education would not dread a day which promised to bring him physically close to Donald Trump, never mind one that was likely to be depicted as demonstrating complicity with him. But he had steeled himself to go through with it as a necessary performance directed towards a more desired end. Moreover, his actual role was planned to be minimal, little more than a momentary pressing of politically disgusting flesh.

It was the tunnel itself which freaked him out. There

was nothing particularly scary about it, to the senses at least, but thinking made it so. As he walked along it he recalled that near the apartment blocks in Glasgow where he had grown up there was truly terrifying old railway tunnel, little more than a tube of corrugated metal screwed horizontally into a small hill adjacent to his local church, which had been the furtive location for successive generations of delinquents to pursue nefarious pleasures: shaggers in the sixties, glue sniffers in the seventies, shooters-up in the eighties, pissers and shitters at all times. Local adolescent lore had it that if you walked through that tunnel you came out the other end with at least one infection, if not several. By comparison, the present tunnel was antiseptic, reasonably lit, its walls professionally finished for the most part, urine- and faeces-free. The problem was its very existence, its being part of a plan precisely to undermine the exercise of public will going on above ground, its deliberate yet furtive facilitation of the institution's continued smooth running in the face of such an obstacle. Governments legitimately required secret passages in the eventuality of enemy attack, owed it to their millions of citizens to keep things going. But to discover that such a construction was being used effectively to ignore mass political protest, in what McNamara still thought of as a publicly accountable institution, appeared to him more than an unsettling development. It was closer to an obscenity in which he was a senior collaborator.

When he walked upstairs through empty corridors and entered Redman's office and began to express some of these reservations, the younger man experienced a little surprise, though he did not evince it. In part Redman was touched to see signs that McNamara's conscience was still alive, though perhaps pulsing only feebly, deep in the cave of office-bearing propriety in which the man seemed recently to have taken abode. But he thought it a bit late in the day for these anxieties, and said so. It would, in any case, he added, all be over soon.

McNamara was listening to Redman with one ear and attending with the other to the constant cataract of crowd noise, like that produced in a football stadium at capacity, seeming to surround the building, pushing through all its gaps and cracks, making its windows periodically vibrate.

Redman continued breezily. "Sit rep. According to the TV news Airforce One will touch down at Birmingham in the next fifteen minutes. Trump will be in the chopper soon enough. Outside on the local barricades the order of play in the next hour, I have discovered, is, firstly, a rousing demagogic performance from Donald Doyle, but it's not close captioned, so hardly anyone will understand it; two, Poon is then going to strut her stuff; three, our local Labour MP is taking a short break from her recently publicised affair with her assistant to contribute her tuppence worth of a speech; but pride of place goes to Yunus and Faraj, who are scheduled to Skype us all from Yunus's detention centre, projected onto massive screens, while Trump is in the building. I think this may deliberately give the false impression that Faraj is somehow also weirdly in custody. I will go outside in time to catch it all. Are you bluetoothed up so I can talk to you freely? We're keeping the line open for the entire hour?"

McNamara nodded. "If it's okay with you."

"Then call me when you're ready," said Redman. He watched as McNamara moved towards the corridor.

"Oh," he suddenly remembered, "Lorraine has an interview for a job at Surleighwick."

McNamara halted. He closed the door and turned around. "Fark," he said. "You've known this for a while?"

Redman shook his head. "Email from her this morning."

McNamara took a few steps forward and, somewhat again to Redman's surprise, resumed his seat. "Hard to blame her feeling that way after what's happened here. Maybe it's not so bad. Surleighwick's only an hour or so away."

Redman returned his look steadily. "There was no consultation. Out of the blue. No invitation to discuss. Moratorium on even talking to her 'til afterwards."

"She might not get the job. It's hardly make or break."

"I'd consult with this *dog* before I applied for a job elsewhere," Redman asserted conclusively.

"The Eagle is in the sky," Spooner smiled at McNamara, tapping his right ear with his index finger. "Forty minutes out."

They were in a robing room behind the stage in the Great Hall, a space devised for the donning of antiquated garments during graduation ceremonies, long abandoned to other purposes since surging student populations had required that such occasions be transferred to the aircraft-hangarish sports centre on the fringes of the campus. Neither of them was dressed in any kind of robe. Both sported recently purchased suits. McNamara, in charcoal black, looked, as he nearly always looked, as though he were attending a funeral. Spooner was in a dapper, eye-catching, tan three-piece number and bow tie, and seemed ready at any moment for a constitutional on a promenade. He was perceptibly relaxed. McNamara, tense, wondered how he managed it.

"We are to begin our proceedings when Trump is five minutes out," Spooner continued. "Apparently my introductory speech is not important enough for him actually to be subjected to it. He just arrives, when I see him in the wings I announce him and give way, he assumes the podium, says something formal and pre-pared, then adlibs some fol-de-rol, you know, the irritating way he does, presents a giant cheque for the sake of the paparazzi, turns on his heel, shakes half a dozen hands in a line, including yours, then pisses off back to the airport. Personally, I think it's all delib-erately choreographed at high speed to create the illusion that giving away forty million pounds is a trivial ninety-second job for him."

McNamara was eyeing the part of the Great Hall he could see beyond the door frame to which Spooner had his back. It was jammed with reporters, microphones, the bright lights of innumerable camera crews, colourful and familiar transnational media logos, University security guards forming a forward cordon on the main floor while Secret Service agents thronged on the stage. It was the biggest show he had ever seen in town. He noted with some irony that not a single student or academic appeared to be among the massed bodies.

"The quicker the better," he said.

Spooner nodded in agreement. "The other PVCs should be here soon. Can you repeat the drill to them, decide on the order of the handshaking line? I have some TV and radio stuff to see to before we start."

As Spooner moved off through the door, Redman's voice sounded in McNamara's earpiece. "Doyle is up."

"He's started?"

"About to. I doubt if there's any real reason to listen, though. I can already paraphrase what he's going to say. *Och, Trump, away ye go back tae America, ya fat cunt. Long live the Odiumgrad militia!*"

McNamara smiled at Redman's half-decent parody. "The Glasgow nyaff's approach to international affairs," he said.

"Nyaff?" Redman repeated.

"A yelper, a complainer," McNamara glossed. "Keep talking to me."

Redman proceeded to maintain a more-than-passable monologue, hardly flagging for half an hour, painting a word picture for his visually deprived audience of one, like a radio commentator at a sporting event. It was more inventive and entertaining than the slightly hysterical and clichéd rants McNamara heard behind Redman's voice, the first in Doyle's rasping vernacular, the second in Poon's downbeat sing-songy, Diane-Abbott-soundalike cadences. Features of the demonstration to which Redman adverted included ethnic diversity, fashion sense, the ratio of women to men and of anarchists to less deluded people, the universal average mental age of the participants (finally estimated, after considerable thought, to be fourteen), coiffure, the banality of mindless chanting, degrees of physical ugliness, and the immoral pressganging of pet dogs (Redman having left his own safely in his office) into a political cause. At the end Redman was actually giving a running commentary on Poon's departure from the stage to preposterously exaggerated roars of acclamation. "And as she climbs gingerly down the makeshift stairs, her ever-fattening arse wobbling like a Chivers jelly, her gait grotesquely deformed by decades-long abuse of Ben Wa balls –"

"Hang on a minute," McNamara interrupted. "Something going on in here."

"Uh-huh. What?"

"Spooner. There's some disagreement between him and the Secret Service *gruppenführer*. It looks like he's starting his address five minutes earlier than planned."

Redman, outside beyond the barricades, was watching the adulterous local Labour MP ascending the steps of the stage and crossing it to the podium when the massive screens behind her, which had shown her head and shoulders momentarily in shot, went entirely dark. She began speaking with her lips to the microphone, but nothing of what she said was amplified. She tapped the mic's windshield, but again the percussion was not heard. She had begun to look around for technical assistance when the vast acreage of flat screen LEDs flickered into life again behind her, but this time unexpectedly showing the head and shoulders of a mightily salubrious-looking Spooner. For a second his face hovered there, smiling, like the good dream version of Big Brother. When he spoke his geniality did not fade, despite the incredible loudness of volume experienced if, like Redman, one was close to the stage.

What he said was, simply, "Good afternoon, ladies and gentlemen."

Crowd noises were sucked away into silence within a second. The intervention seemed to take everyone unawares. The Labour MP turned and leaned backwards and stared up at Spooner's monumentally large face, which loomed over her, the thwarted speaker's head barely reaching the bottom of the on-screen nose.

"Is this part of the plan?" Redman asked, raising a finger to push his bluetooth device further into his ear to counteract the increasing ambient noise. "Spooner is on all the screens. They seem to have been commandeered."

McNamara's reply could not be heard because a sudden explosion of booing and hissing and swearing and name-calling rose up in a deafening crescendo from the crowd and extended itself for ten or fifteen seconds before it began to abate. All the while Spooner's benevolent smile beamed out over the assembly. After one or two further interrupted attempts to begin his speech, and further generous patience on his part, there was a flurry of shushing that eventually permitted him to be heard.

Just before Spooner resumed, Redman heard McNamara say, "It isn't part of any plan I was privy to. He said nothing about broadcasting a speech to the crowd. I thought the speech was for the press in here only."

"When I say good afternoon, ladies and gentlemen," Spooner had begun again, "I mean the ladies and gentlemen outside this building, who I understand can now see and hear me, rather than the invited guests here in the Great Hall where I am speaking. I know that many of you are Odium students and it seems right that I should address you directly. I am aware also that there are many more of you who have come from far and wide and, let's not beat about the bush, you have done so to let it be known how strongly you oppose and wish to protest at today's event. Nonetheless, you are welcome. I should say that, although I cannot see you, I can hear you. You are making an impressively loud noise. Can I just check with you all, though, that you can hear me? If you can hear me will you give me a yes?"

"Lots of puzzlement in the crowd," Redman reported. "Even some amusement, if I'm not mistaken."

The hairs on the back of his neck suddenly stood on end at a ferocious boom of collective affirmation that issued from the crowd: "YES!"

"Fark!" he heard McNamara hiss.

Redman was retreating a few yards for the sake of his eardrums. "You heard that?" He looked at the screen. Spooner's white teeth showed in an amused grin.

"Too right I heard it," said McNamara. "We all heard it."

"Okay, good." Spooner gathered himself. "Now, let me get one thing clear at the beginning. Do you want me to accept this very large sum of money from President Trump?"

"What the fuck is this?" Redman wondered aloud to McNamara. "What's he playing at? This isn't how these things go down."

"No!" bellowed the crowd in unison.

"I have no idea," replied McNamara.

On the screen, Spooner could be seen nodding with pursed lips. "Let me ensure there is no misunderstanding. You do not want the University of Odium to benefit from eighty million pounds of new investment?"

After the briefest of pauses, "No!"

In the slight second of silence that followed an individual male voice somewhere in the mob screamed, "Blood money!"

"Twat," said Redman.

"What?" said McNamara.

"Not you," Redman replied.

"I understand," Spooner was saying. "But I want you to be very firm in your thinking here. It may be that you believe this money comes with conditions. It does not. This University has in the past, before my time, done questionable deals with some donors, I will admit. Many of the staff will remember the scandal around tobacco research three years ago..."

Redman, on a sudden inspiration, pulled his phone out of his pocket. "Robert, is there a BBC camera crew on this? Can you see them in the Hall?"

"Yes," said McNamara in the discreet undertone he had adopted throughout. "They're right at the front. But there are lots of others too."

Redman was tapping quickly on his phone screen. Spooner continued to drone in the background. Redman stamped the sole of his shoe on the ground with impatience as he waited for the 4G connection to buffer. "Shit, yes," he said at last, "it's running live on BBC World. I guess they think Trump is going to walk on any minute. I can see you. Does Spooner think he can persuade this lot to agree with him? Is he mad? Is it a stunt?"

"I really don't know," McNamara responded. "By the way, do I look as if I am talking to someone? Is it obvious?"

"No," said Redman. "You are pretty far in the background and your bluetooth earpiece is not in shot. You could straighten up your shoulders though. You look like a bit of a slouch."

"Our intention," Spooner was saying, "is to use this money, over the next three years, to double investment in the arts, humanities and social sciences. This will mean smaller classes, more staff, and a much larger range of scholarships for students who would otherwise have to pay full fees. We are looking to improve existing facilities and construct entirely new teaching buildings. Mr Trump is making the largest single private donation this University has ever been promised, indeed the largest ever in Britain, with no strings attached. He is not seeking endorsement of his political views or any other kind of influence. Are you really saying that you wish the University of Odium to turn down this offer?"

"YES!" came from the throats of many thousands, but this time the affirmation seemed a tad less fulsome than before.

Redman heard McNamara ask, "That sounded quieter in here. Did it seem quieter to you?"

"Quieter," said Redman, "but not quiet."

"Then you put me in a terrible dilemma," Spooner went on. "Imagine what the consequences of refusing such generosity would be. We live in difficult enough financial times. But you say we should still reject open-handed generosity. That is what you are all telling me? That we should reject it, yes?"

"YES!"

"Quieter still," said McNamara.

"Yes," said Redman. "Is he trying to play them?"

On the screen, Spooner had paused and was looking curious. "Ladies and gentlemen, I'm not sure I heard that this time. Could you just say that again? You want me to reject Mr Trump's money?"

"YES!"

"Now that *was* loud," said McNamara.

"What the fuck?" cursed Redman. "He's, he's –"

Spooner ploughed on. "We live in increasingly isolationist times, and face an uncertain future. Brexit will alter higher education in this country in ways we cannot yet anticipate, but nonetheless you wish the University of Odium to turn its back on a chance to secure its future for the next generation? Is that what you are saying?"

"YES!" came the deafening, concussive response, and then suddenly the word was taken up by the mass as a chant, ever loudening, in quick repetitions, the YESSES bouncing off the walls and the stage and the barricades around, echoing, uttered perhaps in all thirty times until, before it subsided into a general roar of dissolute mass sound, it resembled the regular crack of jackboots on concrete, visually reinforced by thousands of arms punching fists into the air.

Redman's eyes were glued to the screen as the electrifying sonic wave of Trump rejection cascaded over everything and everyone. He watched as Spooner's face altered from its performance of quizzical scepticism to a kind of resigned, yet at the same time slightly amused, acceptance.

"My God," said Redman, "his face."

"I can't see his face," McNamara reminded him.

"He *is* trying to play them," Redman explained. "But I don't think he's trying to play them into agreeing with him. It's like he's playing the ball *to* them, letting it run *with* them, giving it away –"

"I see," said Spooner, and cleared his throat. The look on his face suggested that he was done with any kind of persuasion he may have seemed to have been attempting. "Alright then. The people have spoken. They have effectively said that Mr Trump is not welcome here. I do not believe his helicopter has landed yet and it shall not be allowed to land. Accordingly, henceforth, this building shall not be known as the Trump Building, for it would be an act of gross hypocrisy still to embrace his reviled name. And it behoves me, I believe, to conclude by rendering explicit in words the message which you, the people, clearly wish me to send to the President." His fingers gripped the lectern more tightly and he leaned a little further forward, looking straight into the lens of the camera. *"Mr Trump, you can shove your money up your ass."*

Chapter Fifteen

"What just happened? What the fuck just happened?"

McNamara heard no answer to his question, as Redman was trotting away from the suddenly surging, ecstatic, celebrating mob.

Around McNamara, on the stage and floor of the Great Hall, there had been a short pantomime for several seconds as hundreds of astonished glances were exchanged and palms of hands turned questioningly upwards. He himself was immobile, rooted to the spot, lacking any intuition or instinct as to what to do. The first person he saw act decisively was the American whom Spooner had been talking to earnestly just before he began his speech, one of the President's forward party. The man stalked vigorously towards the exit, passing directly in front of McNamara, his finger on his earpiece, declaring loudly, "Abort! Abort! Do not land The Eagle. I repeat, The Eagle must not land. *Abort!*" Then he was gone.

McNamara felt his elbow gripped tightly. He turned and saw Spooner's face, hot and animated, near his.

"Come with me, now," Spooner demanded. "We have to get out of here. I need to talk to you."

"But —" McNamara began. Then, "What —"

"Go with him," advised Redman telephonically, still in McNamara's ear. "I can still see you both on TV. Go. Find out what you can. Keep this line open. I want to hear what the fucker has to say."

A few moments later McNamara was riding upwards in a nearby elevator with Spooner, with what sounded like an ongoing riot happening in the distance, or hopefully just the orgy of mass celebration. Both men were breathing heavily, and neither had spoken since the doors had closed, but McNamara was amazed that Spooner still seemed less flustered than himself.

"Well," Redman whispered to McNamara, "aren't you going to ask him anything?"

McNamara turned to Spooner, but assuagingly the Vice Chancellor raised his hand. "We'll go up to the top floor, across the building, down in the other elevator to the basement, then into the tunnel," he said. "There we should have uninterrupted privacy. That's where we'll talk. It won't take long."

"Whatever," said Redman, already in his own privacy with McNamara. "Unbefuckinglievable."

McNamara said nothing. The two men walked purposefully along the straights of corridors and around their angles, into another claustrophobic elevator, down, out, through the tunnel entrance door, which was now locked but which Spooner had a key for, which he used, and then used again to lock it on the other side. Then he rested his back against the wall, let out a great sigh of relief, and began to laugh gently.

"I'm sorry about the guilty getaway," he said.

"Getaway?" McNamara repeated. "I didn't see any

robbery to get away from. You didn't get any money."

"More a giveaway," Redman said secretly to Mc-Namara.

"More a giveaway," McNamara repeated to Spooner. "You just turned down eighty million pounds."

Spooner was still chuckling. "Yes, you're right." He reached into his inside jacket pocket and took out a white envelope. A name was written on it in blue ink. "As my Pro-Vice Chancellor of choice, I would be grateful if you would contact the President of the University Council in order to deliver this to him personally. My last request of you."

McNamara looked blankly at the letter, and then again at Spooner.

"Obviously," said Spooner, "it's my resignation."

McNamara heard Redman whistle softly in his earpiece. "It was all planned."

"Why?" said McNamara.

"Why do I want you to give him my resignation letter?" Spooner asked.

"No. Why did you do all this? You prepared the resignation in advance because you intended this to happen, obviously. Everything in the Great Hall was a burlesque, performed for the cameras. You were always intending to refuse the money. Why not just say no all those months ago when the approach was first made? Why put everyone through this? Why drag the University through it, in public? Why make it look as if your decision was spontaneous?"

Spooner's smile seemed ineradicable. "I could give lots of reasons for that, but I can't hang about here for too long if I am going to evade the press. For one thing, it's not every day you find yourself in a position in which you can humiliate the President of the United

States, live on global television. Ordinarily the thought of doing so would also not occur to one, but it is *this* President of the United States I humiliated, this particularly stupid fuckwit. I even refused him landing rights in the building bearing his own name. And I made thousands of people happy by putting his nose out of joint in public. In short, I made a massive point."

"That's it? *You made a point?* You engineered a situation involving thousands and thousands of people, you deceived your staff and students, to lure Trump into an ambush, just to embarrass him?"

"Oh no," Spooner said. "That's not how it looks at all. What everyone saw was me spontaneously obeying the will of the people, and normally disenfranchised people at that, students and youths, whom power-crazed bastards like me and Trump usually ignore completely. What people saw was a Vice Chancellor who's more in the Jeremy Corbyn mould, acting for the many, not the few. What people saw was an example of principled opposition, refusing to allow money to dictate to morality."

"But that's just an illusion. It was none of those things. It was plain suicidal recklessness. Where is the morality in using the entire institution as a dog to be wagged by your tail? Where is the morality in lying to everyone and whipping up this frenzy of political activism?"

"Well, that's easy. I just gave everyone a very good example of the effectiveness of political activism. I just made the myth of the people's will look like a reality. I do, of course, regret the necessary deceptions, and I can see that you object to being lied to yourself, though I find it a bit laughable that you are getting on your high horse about a very predictable thing, a mendacious Vice

Chancellor. Mendacity would seem to me almost a requirement of the job in most cases. My predecessor was certainly no truth-teller, but note how I have helped additionally to erase his obscene legacy, his abject prostration to the market. As for suicide, I am fifty-six and have a pretty full pension pot and an already invested inheritance from a millionaire father. I hardly need to work, haven't *had* to work for a long time. But I did just make myself the best-known University Vice Chancellor on the planet. I just fucked-over *Donald Trump*, seen by many as the most hateful *person* on the planet, almost certainly the most loathed man with significant power. I just harpooned that power. I wouldn't be surprised to be installed as the President of an American Liberal Arts College at twice the salary within a couple of months. I'm surprised my phone isn't ringing already, frankly."

"Robert," Redman said, "there's no point in arguing with him. Nothing can be gained by remonstrating. He's exalted himself in his own head. He thinks he's fulfilled some personal destiny. And it's too late now anyway."

"I even got you out of China," Spooner said. "With profit. Christ, that alone was an achievement."

"I," McNamara said gravely, "am less morally cavalier about deceit than you are."

"Good!" Spooner nodded. "I'm glad to hear it. Because I would think it ninety-nine per cent certain that, ten minutes after this letter is opened, they will ask you to be the Acting Vice Chancellor of the University of Odium while they search for a permanent replacement. The reason I say that is that my letter itself strongly recommends you as the only possible immediate successor. You showed your leadership abilities in China. Play your cards right and you will be the permanent replacement also. I don't see them risking the position again on an unknown quantity, another outsider. And so, I give you that amazing opportunity too. Even if you do consider me immoral, you have the remedy. You *are* the remedy. I have *made* you the remedy. Now will you take the letter, please, because I really have to scram?"

McNamara examined the envelope, the neat cursive script, the polished and rounded thumbnail which rested on top of it, the smooth skin of the hand and wrist disappearing into the outstretched arm of the light brown jacket. He felt a jolt of nausea.

"Robert," said Redman's cool voice in his ear, "take the letter."

McNamara realised he was looking at tarmac, very close up. It was grey, it was hard, it was scarred and ridged, and it was a mere few inches from his eyes. It was also Scottish, though he could not imagine what test would be required to prove this obvious truth. He could feel great pain somewhere, in his lower body, below the waist, a drilling agony that pulsed, came and went, giving momentary relief before it bore into him again. Eventually he localised it in his left hip. Then he felt it in his right hip. He could hear someone talking, standing on the road above him, a gabble of indeterminate language to begin with, but he could not move his neck to see who it was. All he could do was roll his eyeballs, an act which brought into view a pair of black boots which he instantly recognised as his elder son's. This too gave some relief, until the words began to resolve themselves into comprehensible forms, and he heard one side of a conversation he assumed his son must be conducting on a mobile phone.

"Yeah, well," his son was saying, "the car's okay, but dad's a complete write-off. I'm just waiting for someone to come and scrape him off the road, then I'll be on my way again. I should be there in an hour."

The callousness of these expressions stimulated a degree of consternation in McNamara which his body seemed unable to express. He writhed, but all the writhing felt merely internal. No amount of struggle rewarded him with the movement or linguistic articulation which might signify life to any observer. Helplessly, he heard his son say, "Hmm, severed at the thighs, both legs, I doubt if he suffered, but whether or not he did, it's over now, so nothing to fuss about."

A car horn had gone off, blaring repetitively, and getting louder. The toe of one of the boots before his eyes made contact with his shoulder, at first prodding and then more strongly attempting to lever his body over. McNamara had by now got used to the fact that he was dreaming even in advance of awaking, and began to feel relief before the gently rocking hand of Drusilla in the bed next to him and the ringing of his phone had together lured him back into a world where his real son might in fact give a damn about his violent death.

The screen of the phone, which Drusilla held out to him still ringing insistently, read simply, "Unknown number". McNamara took it with a groan.

"Pwoah!" exclaimed a gruff male voice on the other end. "Professor Candelabra, what a long time it's been, such a long time! It's more than thirty years since I listened patiently to all that Marxist guff of yours at Balliol, what?"

McNamara emitted a deliberate snort of indignation before reciprocating. "Boorish, you didn't take any of my classes. I made no contribution to the moderateness of your academic success. I vaguely remembered you from Oxford but I honestly didn't notice you much before you started popping up on telly years later. I do remember the nickname 'Candelabra', devoid of all wit and edge as it was, though I did not associate it with you. Now to what do I owe the displeasure, so early on a Saturday morning? What wrong so grave must I have committed to be punished by a call from you?"

There had been good-hearted chuckling on the line all through this raillery. The reply came, upbeat. "I too have heard 'Boorish' before, but I think I favour 'Bearish' as being more accurate, no? Haw haw. But I hear that congratulations are in order. You are the new Vice Chancellor of one of our Great British Universities. Bravo!"

"Not quite," said McNamara. "I'm *Acting* Vice Chancellor."

"Ah yes, I know, and there's many a slip 'twixt cup and lip, and all that, but still –"

"If I can look forward to calls from you," McNamara interrupted, "no cup will touch my lips at all. I did expect to be contacted by the Higher Education Minister, and so I was, yesterday, which was a work day, not the weekend, and from that point on I expect government intervention in the running of a university to be minimal, occasional, certainly not daily, and never on a Saturday."

"But but but," countered a voice reminiscent of The Goons, "things nonetheless have a tendency to go on happening even on the weekends, do they not? And although I am the Foreign Secretary, and nothing to do, thank the ancient gods, with our wonderful, world-class institutions of higher learning, I did not think it too much to lean upon a personal acquaintance as the basis for a useful discussion of the peculiar, shall we say, geopolitical circumstances in which we find the one you now lead. You're lucky the PM herself isn't on the blower, but she's probably having an early morning fruit tea admixed with her own tears. She considered Spooner an old friend and is probably aghast at his personal betrayal. So playing Atlas to this small world of ours falls to me."

"What," said McNamara, ignoring most of this, "would, in your view, constitute a *useful* discussion?"

"May I be blunt? Well, I shall anyway. A *useful* discussion would be a *fruitful* one. It would bear fruit. It would be one in which you agreed to offer a grovelling public apology to the President of the United States."

McNamara swallowed but did not reply. Seconds passed.

"I mean to say," the Foreign Secretary began again, "on top of the China debacle, in which I understand that you personally dealt the fatal blow, and which, oh, you have no idea, has caused not only damage to the interests of every one of our universities in Asia, but also untold, unimaginable harm to our broader economic relations with that continent, now, only a week later, you blow a huge public rasper at the unbounded generosity of the new President on his first touchdown on our soil since his election. You tell him to shove it, *a posteriori*, as it were."

"Spooner, not me."

"The prior occupant of your office nonetheless."

McNamara sighed. "And if I don't?"

"Well, we shall have to replace you with someone who will. There does have to be an apology, you do understand that?"

"Maybe," said McNamara. "But not a grovelling one. In any case, you'll be lucky to find anyone to replace me. I'm pretty much the last man standing. I will give an explanation and I will use the word *sorry* in respect of the bad manners Spooner exhibited. But there's a small favour I'd like in return."

"Pwah, I don't really think Odium is in a position to bargain!"

"It's really a trivial matter in the scheme of things. It concerns an ex-employee of ours. He's Tunisian."

"Oh, the one arrested on terrorism charges?"

"There were no terrorism charges. He's guilty of nothing except a dodgy passport, and he's about to go to trial for it. This has caused only division and conflict on this campus since it happened. I wondered what might be done short of a trial. A trial will only enflame everything further."

"You'd rather we administratively remove him?"

McNamara sighed once more. "I was rather hoping for something more humane than deportation. Like you finagle him a work permit so that we can reinstate him, and somehow make the illegal immigration charge disappear."

"Pfffffff," exhaled the Foreign Secretary. "Not my department, that. Bit irregular. Damned preferential treatment too, what?"

"Yes," said McNamara. "He's young, impulsive, yet his intentions were not ill: he does not need his life to be ruined by one or two minor acts of folly. And I could do without a local civil war."

"Hmm, hmm," murmured the voice in the speaker. "Okay, possible, but the apology..."

"I won't," McNamara repeated, "apologise for the

refusal of the donation. I will apologise for the manner of the refusal."

"But will you ... grovel?"

McNamara raised fingers to his brow wearily. "If it does the trick, if that's what you really want, then alright."

The bargain was finally concluded and McNamara put the phone aside. He sat back on the pillows and admired Drusilla's naked back as it moved gently with her breathing. He pulled a lock of her hair to the rear of her neck so that he could see something of her face. He felt his loins stir lyrically. He shimmied down and brought the front of his body close to the back of hers, spooning, breathing in her scent, extending his arms to encircle her.

"I bet," he teased, beginning to kiss her shoulder, "you never thought you'd be in bed with the Vice Chancellor of Odium."

He felt her squirm suddenly in his arms. Mistakenly imagining that the reflexive movement was one of desire or pleasure, he did not wait for Drusilla to voice her agreement, and continued without paying attention to the fact that she did not.

"The novel that simply cries out to be a TV mini-series ... the *House of Cards* of the modern British university ... a thrilling satirical exposure of the witless evils of today's academy."

TV FOR TOMORROW

"Clockman has done it again! It's all here: the obloquy which taints all who choose to serve in today's university; the tyranny of social media; Brexit; the banal realities of modern anti-terrorism; even a zombie and ripe evidence that the #MeToo movement is an understatement. I laughed all the way through then wrote my resignation letter."

T(R)OPICAL LITERATURE

"At last Clockman's great comic trilogy is concluded. Quentin Tarantino meets the campus novel in an ecstatic renovation of the genre. Gone is all the humanistic twaddle and intellectual imposture which have beset the depiction of universities in fiction since day one. In their place we get the modern institution in all its cold-blooded malice, mean-spirited calculation, narrow-minded prejudice and, ultimately, maniacal self-destructiveness."

PSYCHOTEXTE

Now available in one volume as *The Odium Trilogy*